THE TEETH OF A
SLOW MACHINE

Andrew Roff was a winner of the 2021 Griffith Review
Emerging Voices Competition, the 2020 Peter Carey Short
Story Award, and the 2018 Margaret River Press Short Story
Competition. His stories have appeared widely, including in
Meanjin, *Island*, *Overland*, *Southerly*, *Westerly*, *Griffith Review*
and *Going Down Swinging*. In 2016 he was shortlisted for
the Wakefield Press Unpublished Manuscript Award at the
Adelaide Festival Awards for Literature. Andrew lives on the
unceded Country of the Kaurna people of the Adelaide plains.

◆

'At turns dreamlike, luminously satirical, fever-pitched and
achingly mortal, the scope of Andrew Roff's debut collection
is utterly refreshing and a joy to linger in. These stories abide
by their own mysterious and persuasive rules, structurally
and stylistically venturous without ever compromising
their racing human and creaturely hearts.'

JOSEPHINE ROWE

THE
TEETH OF
A SLOW
MACHINE

♦

ANDREW
ROFF

Wakefield
Press

Wakefield Press
16 Rose Street
Mile End
South Australia 5031
www.wakefieldpress.com.au

First published 2022

Edited by Jo Case, Wakefield Press
Book design by Duncan Blachford, Typography Studio

ISBN 978 1 74305 891 6

A catalogue record for this
book is available from the
National Library of Australia

Wakefield Press thanks
Coriole Vineyards for
continued support

Contents

Bock Bock

For lunch I ate the wings of three and a half birds. Coleslaw on the side. The local franchisees kept their oil too hot, and it hit my sinuses all rancid and plasticky, a tell-tale sign of polymerisation. Inexcusable, since there's a digital temperature control on the side of the machine. Next time the duty manager bustled past, I held up a nutbrown flake of batter and told him to re-read the manual.

The streetside doors parted, and a swirl of soupy, unconditioned air blew through the service area. Pen kept her eyes forward, pretending she hadn't seen me. In her own time, she returned from the counter doing the fast-food shuffle, balancing two large chips and a soft-drink cup full of gravy on a plastic tray. Penny was new to Dark Meat, transferred about a month ago from Legal, and the keyword perks still gave her a buzz. Good for her, I supposed, but that joy would fade. I didn't think Pen was in this line of work for the right reasons, but no-one got to choose their partner.

'Tell me about the club,' I said.

'I saw the snack list, and it's textbook appropriation. The food isn't bad at all.' She lowered her voice and leaned forward, careful not to let her cream blouse brush the top of the gravy cup. 'If I had to guess, he's started with something close to the Recipe and made tweaks of his own.'

'Did you get a name?'

Pen nodded. 'I found a waitress who was happy to talk. She says he's John Ebner. Goes by Johnny. According to her, he started about six months ago.'

We'd received word about a nightclub. A dive, by reputation, but experiencing something of a revival since they'd started offering a chicken dish called 'JFC'. Word was, most of the patrons weren't there to dance, so you can see why it had fallen to Enforcement.

I unlocked my phone, cursed the technicolour smear my finger left on the screen, and hunted through the pockets of my jacket for a microfibre cloth. I fought a brief, hopeless war against what hangs in the air, oozes from our pores and settles on everything we touch – and ran Johnny's name through our alumnus database. Sure enough: a Jonathan Royce Ebner had juggled vats at a nearby store. Resigned eight months ago. 'Lines up,' I said.

For the most part, Pen knew what she was about. She was in her early thirties. Buxom, not legitimately fat like me. Pleasing to the eye, but her bearing discouraged anything unprofessional. Hair yanked tight and pinned, suit-squeezed, a creature of business who still dressed for her last job. She was careful with her words, and quick to make the kind of connections that were important. But watching her eat, I saw another side. She sucked the gravy-limp potato straws into her face like they were spaghetti, leaving evidence on her lips and chin.

I looked down at the benchtop, at her close-trimmed fingernails spattered in brown. 'We'll have to pay him a visit,' I said.

Pen stopped chewing. Went to speak, hesitated, gulped mightily, took in air, tried again. 'Poor John.'

'Wipe your face,' I said.

◆

Secrets are only secrets if you work to keep them that way. Penny and I are with Enforcement Special Wing, Dark Meat Division. The kind of work we do is covert, but not unique. All the quick service restaurants have their own teams.

Intellectual property theft is a serious matter. Trying to pass off as an authorised franchisee is against the law, but more to the point, it's a falsehood. The least we can do as merchants, as consumers, is to transact and eat with honesty. The birds are honest with us. Cow is beef. Pig is pork. But Chicken is chicken is chicken.

I put in a call to Rufus. I don't know his real name, or anything about him, and fair enough. Penny chose her handle when she joined Dark Meat, and Dixie isn't what the priest called out the day I was baptised. Such details are irrelevant: you judge a person by their actions. Our chief reckons Rufus must be with the cops, but he could just as easily work for one of the giant data-suckers, or the electoral commission. Like always, he stuck to the protocol, picking up after three rings, avoiding chit-chat. 'What sound does a happy bird make?'

'Bock bock,' I answered, supplying the new password.

'What have you got for me?'

I gave him Johnny's name and approximate age. Two minutes later, I felt the thrum of a text against my hip. An address, some place up north.

We'd let Johnny marinate for a couple of weeks. Pen said she'd spoken to a waitress; if we moved too fast, the girl might draw a link. In the meantime, there were plenty of other leads to work.

◆

We arrived in a rented panel van not long after five am, and the line to get into the market stretched almost into the next suburb. Pitch black. Drizzle sank reluctantly through still air, invisible until it strayed into the arc of a street light or one of the spots rigged above the front gate. In the back of the van were two trestle tables and nothing good in the way of stock. But there'd be more trash than treasure at this thing, and all we had to do was look plausible.

When the gates opened, the situation became fluid. The regulars must have slept in their trucks, and now they hopped kerbs and raced to claim territory near where the coffee carts would set up, or down the end of a row. I parked in one of the paint-marked squares towards the centre of things, and for a while Pen and I sat undisturbed, watching the gloom lift as someone turned the dimmer switch on the sky. Like me, Pen had dressed down for the occasion, the edges of her frame unguessable beneath a large hoodie. By seven, our little operation was lost in a jumble of traders ready to hawk flowers, bread, bicycle parts, compact discs, bric-a-brac, jewellery, wood carvings, pears individually sheathed in styrofoam netting, appliances, beef jerky, and straight-up junk.

Before the punters were allowed in, before the sun had properly risen, I left Pen and began to circle, pacing the rows in my tracky dacks and old sandshoes, always taking care to look like I was on my way to somewhere else. Because it amused me to do so, I imagined what it might be like if I'd come here to steal, what I'd be on the lookout for. Rubes, probably. People who should have held a garage sale. Frowning middle-aged women flogging off what was left of their parents' estates. They'd be distractable, and they wouldn't tie the valuable stuff to a board or put it behind glass.

Penny and I were really here to check out reports of a vendor selling T-shirts, to which the likeness of our esteemed Founder had been applied. He'd been depicted performing a sex act on an animal. Needless to say, it was a flagrant breach of certain trademark rights derived from our Founder's image.

What makes my blood boil is contempt shown towards a maker. The Founder conceived the Recipe, a wonderful gift to the whole world. There are always people who want to tear down the reputations of others. There is no greater crime, and I know what I'm talking about because I've been to divorce court. I've stood fuming at the bench while they lied and lied; the most shameful untruths. Now my kids hear it second-hand, and whatever I do or say for the rest of my life, and even after I'm gone, they'll never be sure.

But the market – I had time to kill, and I used it to learn the character of the place, the layout, so that later it would feel like I was monitoring everything from a surveillance camera, and I could wander between stalls with my eyes closed if I wanted to. I watched a group of teenage girls sort second-hand clothes onto hangers. The girls wore ribbons in their hair, and matching rugby jumpers with white collars. Far too bubbly for the hour, they huddled together oblivious, chattering, like prey.

'. . . And they live together, on opposite sides of the line, half a house each.'

'That's got to be fake.'

'Nuh-uh, I read it on *Buzzfeed*. It's real, they quote her.'

Why were they flogging their mums' French Connection? Why here, and not online? School fundraiser most likely, for charity or a new annex for their boatshed. Taking up position behind a stack of second-hand books, I watched as a lean old woman, bitter with private history, descended on the group. She snatched up an armful of dresses, as many as she could hold, and approached one of the kids. After a short, sharp negotiation, the lady handed over a twenty. Briskly, she returned to her own set-up three stalls away, dumped her purchases on a table, re-priced them, and hung them up on racks, everything old becoming new again. One of the girls, sour-faced now, split off from the herd and approached, waving the red note in the air, attempting to unwind the transaction, but it wasn't on. Fair enough, too. Those kids had been selling their stock for well below market, and that's bad business.

At eight o'clock the hoi-polloi were let in, and I circled back to make sure Pen had finished setting up our stall. One of the interns in local Enforcement must have been sent down to a pawn shop, and swept some random crap into a basket, and now we exhibited an eclectic mix of wares: a ukulele, some scarred brooches, a pair of sneakers, a painted egg thing, and plastic folders stuffed with basketball cards. Penny looked cold, slouched low in a fold-out seat. She was eating a pretzel, taking hurried bites as she made conversation with prospective customers. 'Remember why we're here,' I told her.

Utilising our cover, I took time to speak with our neighbours. Asked for advice, admired their stock, and wondered aloud whether they might remember anyone selling 'funny'

T-shirts. Irreverent, pop-culture stuff. Maybe there were famous people depicted in compromising positions, stuff like that. I bought some shit I didn't need, that no-one could ever need, to try to grease the wheels.

We packed up at lunchtime, empty-handed. Perhaps the culprit had moved on, or maybe the tip was fake news, fed to us by a rival chain just to waste our time. They've done that kind of thing before, and we've done it to them, too. But we can't quit; every season brings more violators, and we pull them up like a farmer pulls weeds. Or, if you prefer: the deceitful are like moths to the flame. Birds to the easy grain. Whatever floats your boat. Bock bock.

◆

Every day stumbles into the next, swearing and turning over tables as it falls. When we travel, they put us up in miserable hotels. Mid-rise concrete boxes looming over the suburbs like an affront. Couldn't have been built more than a decade ago, but somehow the grey carpet has always worn threadbare. Watercolour prints of flowers on the walls that are so deliberately, aggressively bland, you can look at them and feel your blood pressure rise. Nowhere comfortable to sit. Nothing in the mini-fridge. Low-draw LEDs that flicker an ache into your head.

I can't stand those places, so in between jobs, I get out. You can gather a lot of intel on foot. Sometimes I pass one of our chain's 800+ convenient Australian locations, and calculate traffic conversion rates at dinnertime. More than once I've wandered shopping districts, inspecting collateral for cafes and takeaway joints, and noted minor infringements, fodder for the letter-writers in General Enforcement to sort out.

On the night before we paid Johnny a visit, I was moving slow. The sun was struggling against the horizon's pull, and a hot wind had kicked up, and I could feel grit accumulate on my person. Framed in the sky against the dusk, I saw the shape of a being with large, flared, feathered wings. It might have been an angel, and I watched it for a few minutes, but it just seemed to be cruising around.

After strolling for more than an hour through quiet suburbia, I rejoined a major arterial road that would take me back to my goddamned hotel. Pushed by a gust, I came to a side street, and observed ahead of me a large red sedan, stopped at the intersection to make a right-hand turn onto the main road. A woman, early to mid-twenties, who I would describe as of South Asian appearance, was approaching from the kerb opposite me. She checked for other traffic, and walked in front of the vehicle to cross the road. The sedan lurched forward, hitting the woman above the knee and sending her sprawling. The car jerked to a stop, backed up, swerved past the victim, and peeled out down the main road.

I helped the woman pick herself up, got her back to the footpath. She'd scraped her left arm when she'd landed, but I couldn't see any other injuries.

It didn't make sense. There had been no need, she would have been out of the way in seconds, and the car could easily have made the turn. It had to have been deliberate.

'I saw everything,' I said. 'I've got the licence plate.' Even as

I spoke, I was typing a note into my phone, jabbing at the tiny keys on the screen. 'I'll call the police.'

'No, no,' the girl protested. I asked her if she was sure, and she said she was. 'But . . .' She pulled out a piece of paper with a street address on it, and a bus stop number.

Together we figured it out. She had another kilometre to walk. She nodded at me once, unsmiling, and set off. I watched her go, and saw the limp she was trying to hide.

There's so much injustice in this world, and most of it goes unpunished, and that's why you have to look out for yourself on the roads.

◆

Ever since that call with Rufus, I'd been thinking about the new password. *Bock bock*, the sound of a happy bird. Something even a child knows. Children know important things, and even better, they are ignorant when it comes to some of life's harsh realities. I've seen how our product is grown; they locked me in one of those airless sheds for three hours. The stench almost made me vomit, but I kept breathing and I held it inside because I knew it was a test, to make sure I am made of the right stuff to guard the Recipe. More than the smell, it was the sound that got to me. Thousands of creatures under permanent stress make a noise I can't explain. There was too much time, and I came to understand that what had first seemed like a flapping, shrieking tumult was really a sum of moments, as animals fought for space, or plucked themselves, or ground their beaks to salt against the jagged lips of the cage.

Pen got the shed treatment a week before her transfer to Dark Meat, and since then I'd never seen her eat bird. That was probably something I should have reported, but I remember what it was like. It took me a while, too, and I kept thinking, I'll give her another week. In no time she'll be crunching golden skin, and sucking juice from her fingers.

Well-cooked chicken is a treat, and anyone who says otherwise is a liar. I will concede that the joy of eating is not uncomplicated. For me there is shame, too, and that must have something to do with my upbringing. Jesus said, I am the Truth, and every Sunday morning as a boy, as I walked back to my pew, I would hold the wafer gently between my teeth until it disintegrated, wondering what I ought to feel as I consumed His flesh.

Sometimes I have misgivings, but what I do is protective. An act of love. For our product, for our company. Anyone can love a person. I hope you understand.

◆

Johnny lived in a mean upstairs apartment in a yellow-bricked, flat-roofed block of six, so the fruits of his labour couldn't have been all that sweet. Penny and I were patient, watching residents come and go. Long after the sun went down, we observed Johnny parking his old shitbox in the shared carport and trudging up the stairwell, letting himself in.

In the small hours, we approached the target's dwelling and I knocked on his door, my gloves muffling the sound to some extent. It didn't take long for Johnny to open up. He looked like he hadn't been sleeping. Before he could become agitated, I shoved a rag in his face, and he slumped.

'Help me.' Pen picked up the kid's legs and we lumbered inward, flopping him on a coffee-coloured sofa that had seen better days. Moving carefully but with haste, I closed the front door and returned, switching off the television. For the most part, the interior was grimy in a way that has to be earned through time and too many cycles of dirty-clean, a beat set by quarterly inspections and a succession of uncaring tenants. Beanbags and cushions squatted haphazardly on the shag, and an aroma of stale cannabis complemented a selection of audio-visual media and video-game consoles distributed at random across the flat surfaces. It was a surprise when I glanced into the kitchen and registered the stainless-steel gleam of the sink, free of detritus. Pans dangled from hooks installed next to the backsplash. And on the bench, a toaster huddled next to a cubic deep fryer, like a supplicant kneeling before a king.

Johnny moaned groggily. The skin below his mouth shone, dotted with acne and uneven stubble. Man enough, I thought, to choose his path. His dark-brown eyes, when they opened, suggested sorrow, but that might have been the lingering effect of the chloroform.

Before Johnny could recover enough to squirm away, I administered the paralytic. Pen stood distant and still, letting me do all the work.

The paralytic was a vital tool. To an under-resourced coroner (there is no other kind), it is undetectable, a unique formula developed in-house. It wasn't something we advertised, but the company had Recipes for all sorts of things.

Johnny's eyelids fluttered and with difficulty, he parted his lips, letting out a croaking sound. We could begin.

'John Ebner, we are enforcement officers representing your former employer. It has been alleged, and we have confirmed through our investigations, that you did knowingly exploit confidential information – specifically, a trade-secret formula for the preparation of fried chicken – in breach of continuing restraints under your contract of service. Furthermore, you countenanced the sale of offending products under branding that falsely implies approval or endorsement by, or a connection with, your former employer.'

Johnny jerked his head to the side, but did not respond in any coherent way to the charges. That was fine. Through his deeds Johnny had proven himself to be a liar, and his words had no probative value.

I glanced again into the kitchen, let my eyes play over the recipe books stacked lovingly, spines out and flush against the edge of the nook above the microwave. I said, 'You were trying, I can see that. Perhaps you thought you had something to contribute. But the way you went about it – you didn't pay those birds any respect.'

A gurgling sound repeated from Johnny's windpipe, and for an instant I imagined he was trying to say, *Bock bock*. But that was ludicrous. Johnny was not a bird, and Johnny was not happy. From my backpack I fished out a pack of durries and a plastic soft-drink bottle filled with colourless fluid. I wedged a cigarette between Johnny's twitching fingers, his hand dangling over the edge of the sofa. The rest of the pack I left open on the coffee table, and I started splashing liquid this way and that.

Johnny strained to make himself understood. 'Nnnnngh.'

Pen said, 'Dixie, look. He's terrified. I don't think he'll sell bad chook again.'

'I know he won't,' I told her.

'Can't we give him a chance?' Penny moved in close now, cupped her hands around the bottle, and drew it slowly towards herself.

'No,' I said, and pried her hands away. 'If you go to bed greasy, you wake up cooked. It's the only thing that works.'

'I know, but—'

I closed the distance between us, until I could feel her breath against my neck. 'If you don't shut up and help,' I said, staying calm, 'I swear I'll put you next to him. I can make it look like a sex thing got out of hand. Where's the lighter?' For a second Penny didn't move, and maybe she was thinking this over. Just as I was growing impatient, she took a step back and opened the front pocket of her bag.

If you're the sort of person who reads the newspaper, then you'll have seen articles about idiots falling asleep smoking and burning themselves alive. In actual fact, that hardly ever happens. What's usually happening is justice.

Penny knelt down and ran her gloved hand over the kid's brow. She picked up the cigarette, lit it, and held it to Johnny's mouth for a time. His slack-lipped panting woke an orange glow. Stepping carefully, Penny moved behind the sofa and tossed the cigarette. We were outside and back to the car before the front window blinds caught.

I started the engine, but Penny wouldn't settle. She kept buckling and unbuckling her seatbelt, reaching for the door handle and then thinking better of it. I waited until the electricity went out of her.

'What is wrong,' she said, and it didn't sound like a question.

Her eyes were on the road, and it felt strange to me, and perhaps to her, too, that we weren't moving.

Pigface

'Sorry – I wouldn't touch that.' They were standing in the dunes, and Kat was trying to watch all six of them. 'It'll give you a rash.'

Gary's fingers were ready to snap a limb off the low, grey-green bush he'd been inspecting. 'You just tell me what ones I shouldn't touch,' he said, dropping his arm. 'And the ones Kev shouldn't eat.'

Ted and Dianne, Kevin and Hitomi, Gary and Sharon. The most important thing was not to forget. You had to use last names for Americans, but this group was from New South Wales. The day before, Kat had tried out *Gaz and Shaz*, but that hadn't been well received.

She got them moving up the hill, away from the beach and the atrium. A raised timber boardwalk led into the bush. In another few hundred metres they would turn on to a patchy dirt trail, switching back to trace the cliff line. A nature walk, to settle the stomach. To give the guests something to do between lunch and canapés.

Dianne stayed close the whole way up. Yesterday she'd seen a tiger snake coiled tight on a granite sunbed, and now she bent forward as she walked, head bobbing, assessing one side of the path and then the other as she placed her feet, like a chook. Behind her, Sharon watched with narrowed eyes, a scrawny old duck too tough for eating. Hitomi might have been a brolga, or a sarus crane. The men were cassowaries: volatile, ugly and proud. Ted the proudest. 'Don't stress,' said Kat. 'With this many people making this much noise, we won't bump into any snakes. They're more scared of us—'

'. . . Than we are of them? Hmph.'

Kat tugged at the bottom of her shirt. The park ranger outfit they'd bought for her was too tight around the bust. Her boss said that she looked legit. She'd thanked him, but back in her room, changing her clothes, she'd thought: *I* am *legit*.

She set a sympathetic pace. Kevin was already complaining about how spiky the plants were. The track was narrow and they'd been advised to wear long trousers – it had been underlined on the daily plan delivered to their rooms – but here they were. Kevin, pot-bellied, top-heavy in a rugby jumper and shorts, was getting his shins scratched.

To distract him, she crouched by a patch of little succulents. 'This is pigface. If you pick up a clump and squint, maybe you can make out the shape of a pig's head.' They did as she suggested. Thick triangular leaves splayed out from a squat green nub. The leaves ran a gradient from light green at the base to deep pink. A startling pink: the most lurid colour in the whole landscape. 'The leaves are sacrificial. The wind here blows up salt spray from the ocean. This place is too exposed for anything else to grow, but these leaves absorb all the salt, getting pinker and pinker, so that the rest of the plant can thrive. Eventually the leaves die off and get replaced.'

Ted stabbed a question at her. 'Latin name?'

'*Carpobrotus rossii.*'

'Is it edible?' Kevin asked, ignoring the groans of the others.

'Actually, yes, it is. You can hold the bit in the middle like this, and suck out the pulp. But it's the wrong season, so they'll be bitter.'

'When can we eat something? Bush tucker.'

'You'll be having muntries in your appetiser tonight. They're berries that grow further inland. A bit sour, like cranberries.'

Kat didn't understand how Kevin could be hungry. They got five square meals a day here. Lunch and dinner were degustations, and their suites were kept stocked with chocolate and cheese.

At the top of the cliff, they watched the sea. The wind ran at them, howling. The wind had formed this landscape of rock and squat, stubborn shrubs. It hurled salt, left every living thing hardened or broken. The sun loitered cold and small, doing what it could, but the wind came up from the Antarctic. Behind the others, Kat closed her eyes and tried to imagine being as old as the land.

Back the way they'd come, the big glass atrium of The Bay caught the light, interrupting the gentle sweep of the beach. Two bent lines of guest rooms stuck out either side, cresting the dunes, each room with an unobstructed sea view. Each couple had paid more for this weekend away than Kat had earned in the last six months.

From up here you could see the swells arrive and break, inevitable but irregularly spaced and sized, so that you had to keep watching to see what would happen next. Mute, apart from the wind.

'Magic,' Sharon pronounced. 'You're very lucky.'

'Yes,' said Kat.

'How long have you been working here?'

'Coming up on a year now.'

'What did you do before?'

'A science degree, then honours in zoology. I tried to get a job at a zoo, but there's a lot of competition.' Kat skipped over the intervening years; happy years of travel and surfing and wait-ressing. 'I came to the island on holiday – I wasn't staying *here*, of course – and I heard there was a position going.'

'You're very lucky,' Sharon said again. Gary, in his white shirt and cream linen pants, nodded and squeezed his wife's hand.

Kat smiled. 'Shall we push on? We're headed to that rise up there.' She turned and picked out her next footfall. There was only a metre between the track and the sheer cliff edge, which made the walk thrilling even if you'd done it a hundred times. She knew that her guests would be looking at the dirt, worried about tripping, eyes flicking up now and then to remind them-selves of what they'd come to see.

'There should be a railing,' Dianne said. 'It's not safe.'

'Where's your spirit of adventure?' said Gary.

Sharon slapped her husband on the shoulder. 'Dianne's right. It's irresponsible.'

Ted, who'd been quiet during the walk, spoke up. 'I'll have a word to the owner.' The way he said it signalled a closing off, like the end of a team meeting. He was a compact man, with an immaculately trimmed moustache that made him look older than he probably was. Helping in the kitchens that morning, Kat had heard that Ted was one of the wealthiest guests ever to have visited The Bay, which was saying something. He'd made his fortune through aluminium. Mining it, or purifying it or something – the kitchen staff weren't sure. Kevin and Gary were merely rich. They'd been described as Ted's business associates, whatever that meant. Kat wondered if she could ever learn to talk like Ted did, leaving no room for dissent.

The next time the path widened, Hitomi drew alongside. 'Excuse me. You live here? At The Bay?'

Kat had been warned about this when she'd started. *Some guests – not all of them, but some – will want to know where you stay, how much you earn, whether you're happy here. Put yourself in their shoes: they can't enjoy themselves if they're feeling conflicted.*

'We don't sleep in the main building, but there's accommodation for staff just a bit further inland. It's nice. We've got televisions, a ping-pong table – everything we need.' Each night, after the last guests had spilled from the lounge bar back to their rooms, Kat returned to the converted shipping container she shared with Francis, the bookkeeper. Kat was sick of the other girl's smell. She'd never seen Francis change her socks.

As they advanced, Kat rattled off trivia about the island. The cliffs jagged eastward, jutting like the teeth of a slow machine, and the ocean made Kat think of the beach five or six teeth ahead, where the staff could swim out of view of the guests. Even in the middle of summer, the water was shockingly cold. In winter, Kat had the place all to herself. With her wetsuit on, she would brave the Southern Ocean in quick stints. She'd heard there was a shipwreck in that water: a fat supply vessel that had arrived in the old days and never left. She'd get some diving equipment together one day.

That beach was the best thing about this place. The beach and the animals: the echidnas, single file on a march; and the whales and kangaroos and feral peacocks and inbred koalas. When she was out by herself, she didn't think about the staff compound. She didn't remember twelve-hour shifts, six days a week, washing windows and chopping vegetables in the kitchen when she wasn't leading walks. Besides, there was nothing else to do with her leisure time. On her day off, she could catch a ride into the nearest town, a half-hour drive away, but all that was waiting was a pub and a petrol station. There was no-one to meet. Fraternisation with other staff at The Bay was a sack-able offence, and the locals were mostly old farmers. Months earlier she'd had a fast, fumbling session with an agribusiness consultant in the back of his ute, but she decided afterwards that it hadn't been worth the trouble.

She missed all the surfers she'd known, except for maybe one or two. She hadn't been back to the mainland since she'd started working at The Bay. Forget the charter flights that brought in the guests — even the ferry was too expensive for an unneces-sary trip. Sometimes, at night, breathing in Francis, Kat thought about leaving.

She gathered them at the point, on top of a big, flat granite rock, and they made a survey. The park in which they stood car-ried well over the horizon. Apart from The Bay and the walking trail, there was no human sign. Kat pulled a pair of binoculars from her rucksack and offered them to Dianne, who accepted them warily, like they might have been a trick.

Boulders and scree spilled in a ramp down to sea-smoothed rocks where the waves smashed. Gary set about making a descent, shirt flapping. Kat had to fight the urge to scramble after him. She tried a warning. 'Careful, Gary. Please. We'd hate to have to call the rescue chopper.'

'I'll be right,' he shouted back up, over the wind.

'Just ignore him,' said Sharon. 'He'll do what he wants, anyway.'

'He's an adventurer,' said Kevin. 'He's intrepid.'

Kat took a half-step back, angling so that she could keep watch. She had a sick feeling and she wanted to make Gary come back. But if she did that, he'd be sure to complain to her boss. Management wouldn't garnish her pay – that was too blatantly illegal – but next month they would find a way to charge Kat extra for her room and board. More than Francis, even though they shared. They'd done it before.

To the rest of them, she said, 'I've got something special to show you. Do you see that island?' She pointed at a dark mass of rock near the centre of the cove, on the far side of the point. No more than five metres at its widest, shoving itself up high out of the water. Moss grew in patches at the top, with a tuft or two of stunted grass. The point took all the force of the ocean, so waves lapped rather than broke inside the cove.

'Two eastern ospreys live there. These guys are the southernmost breeding pair in the world. They're endangered, and very easily disturbed by humans – they'll abandon their nests if they feel threatened. So that rock is a pretty good situation – isolated and protected.'

Hitomi peered through the binoculars. 'I don't see—'

'Here.' Ted snatched the binoculars and fiddled with the thumbscrew.

'They might be off hunting,' said Kat. 'Or hunkered down. Laying season's just finished, so we're crossing our fingers that there are eggs in that nest. We won't know for a while yet.'

From the bottom of the point, Gary called. Everyone turned to watch as he clambered up a slick rock.

'Don't look at him,' said Sharon. But they were all looking now – eyes fixed on the next swell.

'Oi!' Kevin shouted, and tried to point past Gary, to warn him. But Gary didn't understand. When the wave came, he was knocked flat on his face. It felt like there should have been a slapping sound as he hit, or a crack, but not at this distance. Foam covered him, and Kat wondered if he'd be there when the water cleared.

'Shit,' someone said behind her.

Somehow Gary had stuck flat to the rock; a mollusc. After the water drained away, he found his feet. He looked behind, turned to them and gave a sheepish wave and a thumbs-up. He started to climb back.

Kat watched him longer than anyone. When she remembered the rest of them, it was because she heard Ted say, 'If they're in there, I'll wake them up.' Twisting, she saw that he had picked up a large stone. Before she could call *stop*, he pelted it.

Kat followed its arc. She let go a breath, and later she remembered making a noise, *ah*, as she realised that the rock was on its way, and nothing would change that.

It was a decent throw, and almost made the distance to the nest, but hit the water about three metres short. Ted grinned at her, a naughty schoolboy, daring her to tell him off. He laughed.

'Should've put more on it.' He cast around for a partner in crime. Not finding anyone, he faltered. Hitomi couldn't hide her disgust.

'They're endangered, mate,' Kevin said.

Ted's eyes flitted to his wife, who was shaking her head. He made a quick calculation and moved closer to Kevin. 'Let's face it, mate: we didn't come all this way for the exercise. With the amount we're paying . . .' Ted trailed off. There would have been silence, if the wind had allowed it.

Gary had found his way back. Drenched and not bothering to read the mood, he shouted, 'Every day, I am born again!' He raised his arms high above his head, and in his sopping whites, he did look like he'd been baptised. No-one acknowledged him. More quietly, he asked, 'What did I miss?'

'The fun police up here don't like me throwing things off the cliff.'

Dianne said, 'That's not the issue.'

Kat let the wind take her first angry impulse, take her loathing. She felt the hot sting of the sun on the back of her neck. Her forearms were turning bright pink. Pink like pigface leaves on a rise above the ocean, collecting lethal salt.

Once upon a time, on a different coast, an ageing hippy had taught her an incantation. He'd told her it was ancient Sumerian, that it banished negative energy. Kat tried it now, collecting the syllables in her mind. *An. Imin. Bi*, she mouthed, and inhaled through her nose. *Ki. Imin. Bi*. Out loud, she said, 'It's coming up on cocktail hour. I know that the kitchen's been working hard for you guys. We'd better head back.'

'Hold on,' said Ted. 'I want to find the ospreys.'

'Come on, Ted, I could go a G and T. All this nature's made me thirsty.'

'I'm bloody freezing, Ted. I need a hot shower. Come on.'

Ted gazed at the nest, chin out, stubborn as an old explorer. But Dianne had had enough, and she gave her husband a look, and Ted allowed himself to be persuaded. Over dinner tonight they'd laugh about all this. *Did you see the look on Gary's face when he almost got washed out to sea?*

The return journey was quicker. They'd taken in the view on the way up, so they didn't linger. Sharon was complaining that the pillows in her suite were too soft, and that triggered a debate about mattresses.

When they found the path for the beach, Kevin tore off a clump of pigface and squeezed it into his mouth. Kat studied him and began a silent count. Before she got to four, Kevin was spitting pulp onto the sand.

'You were right about the taste,' he said.

Early Adopter

One, two, three running jumping hops and I launch into the sky, wings beating down hard, plastic feathers scraping car park gravel. It's easier with a platform to leap from, but just like the brochure says, you can get *Aloft Anywhere*™ with the *Ascenze Icarus*.

I flap flap flap for altitude and speed. Twist to avoid powerlines. Weird how true the wings are. They follow my arms after the tiniest lag. Faithful, doing so much work, battering the air to keep me borne.

I cruise over the foothills, heading southward, gaining height. Clear day. Off to my right I see the low medium highrise of the city centre, and beyond that the airport, and Anzac Highway turning a dogleg at the racecourse. The world stops past West Beach: sea and sky form a wall.

The wings are ridiculous, dangerous. Dale, the Ascenze sales rep, he told me as much last time we talked, after I paid. He said I'm brave. Told me he's proud of me. Dale's a great guy. *The trick to surviving*, he said, *if there is a trick, is to find a safe flight level and stay there.* Too high, or too close to an airfield, and you get sucked into a jet engine. Too low, and birds – real birds – and drones can be a problem. There have been fatalities in the USA. Mostly people doing stupid stuff like chasing tornados.

I try a few swoops, tuck my wings in close to my body and fan them as I gather speed into the dive. Cockatoos wheel and break, disturbed by the silhouette I cast above them in the blue sky.

It's just me up here. Just me. There aren't any mourners or lawyers or concerned family friends. Mum is a long flight northeast, rattling around in our old house, practising her own glide on a supply of antidepressants. We're both doing what we need to, and no-one else has the right to judge. People are entitled to their opinions, but— but—

Beautiful, these wings, just like the brochure said. *A feat of engineering! A marvel of aesthetics!* And Dale was right; airborne, I hardly feel the power pack behind my shoulder blades. That's the real game-changer, that battery. For centuries, all those would-be birdmen ran into the same problem: to get something as heavy as a human off the ground, you need gigantic wings, seven or eight metres each from shoulder to tip. But if you make wings like that, human muscles aren't strong enough to shift them. Adding a conventional motor just increases weight. A spiral of failure, until the power pack came along. Now, every day brings something new.

Small – smaller than a briefcase stuffed with probate documents. Light – lighter than a textbook for a failed university course. There's enough stored energy on my back to run one of those houses down there for a month. On either side are two pistons feeding into wing spars, tethered to my biceps to copy the movement of my arms. When I flap, the wings flap. If I drop my left arm a fraction – like this – the left wing adjusts, and I bank into a graceful turn.

Oh wow, I'm really moving now. Thank god for this hood. It covers my eyes my ears my hair. It makes me look like a hawk missing its beak. I wiggle my feet in the big heavy boots, strapped into big metal claw feet. These are a gimmick, I know, but Dale recommended them; he's old but he's a good guy. He really likes me, he smiled and put his hand on my shoulder when he said goodbye. The metal feet add weight to the system, but to anyone watching from the ground they complete the look. A giant bird is up here, surveying, circling. And the pneumatic shock absorbers are protective if there's a rougher-than-usual landing.

From up here, houses sprawl like Lego spilled on a kitchen floor. I like it up here but it's too far away. I want to get close enough to see faces, maybe frighten some kids. These bird suits are so new, so expensive, that there are only four of them in the whole country. That's what Dale said. So new that the regulator hasn't made any rules about where or how I can fly. *Total freedom, the sky is yours,* he promised, at least for right now, and I mean to take advantage.

I bare my teeth in a grin as I descend, air buffeting lips and tongue. I let loose a loud cry like a warning to my prey: *caw, caw,* but it's lost to the wind. I'll write to Ascenze Customer Care and tell them to add a microphone and loudspeaker to the next model. At least some sort of horn. Maybe a button you can press to blast out *Ride of the Valkyries.* They'll listen to me, I'm more than a customer. I'm a beta tester. My Opinion is Greatly Valued.

I flatten into a fast glide about forty feet above street level. Stretched out, I cruise above and watch my shadow, wingtips sliding over the footpaths on either side of the road. I get a momentary glimpse of a woman below looking up at me, scowling, giving me the finger, and then I'm past her. Dogs let out high-pitched panicked barks.

Bloody hell the feeling of speed this close to the ground is something else. I tilt a little and bear towards Shepherds Hill, but as I do so I hit some pocket of air. No: a pocket of *no* air, a low-pressure zone. I lose the lift, dip. Hurtle forward fast, ground comes falling up!

I flare wings and flap hard forward and down, bleeding speed, working to correct. An ugly bungalow leaps at me, yellow-brick with a tiled roof. I'm falling too fast, there's no way to avert. Lean back, gather legs under me, brace for impact. Claw feet hit first, crunching near the roof's peak, tearing a hole and cracking the tiles all around. Shock absorbers take the bulk of the force, but still my feet feel like they've smacked concrete. Right wing curls against the front wall of the house. I hope like hell I haven't done any structural damage to the suit. You wouldn't believe what they charge for maintenance on these things but I guess it makes sense, it's all carbon fibre and advanced composite materials and there's only a couple of guys here who are trained to work with that stuff.

It takes a while to get my breathing under control. Stop shaking so bad. I see an old man come scurrying outside and for an awful moment he looks like my dad. But then he starts to shout something and he doesn't sound anything like my dad, and I can move again and I decide it's time to be on my way. Clomp clomp along the spine of the roof until I come to the end. I launch, flapping back into the blue.

◆

When I'm safe up high, I spend a while turning figure eights. I've been reckless, I know that. *Reckless and stupid.* It's Dad's voice I'm hearing. Or the voice of my accountant, who told me not to buy the wings. My share of the estate was just enough to cover the cost, but they're – what did he say? – frivolous. A depreciating asset. And me with no job. Should I have offered to pay the old man for the damage I did to his roof? But I'm two suburbs away now and it'd be hard to find the house again.

It's calm up here. It's lonely up here, but that's okay. As an only child, I'm used to being alone. All smart people feel alone, and I'm smarter than anyone gives me credit for. Some people are destined to be scientists, librarians. There are healers, guides, philosophers. Enforcers. I am a man of leisure. *Everything we've given you, you've wasted. But I'd rather you were a happy failure than a miserable success.* My dad. The last, nicest thing he ever said.

No-one gives me any credit. What the ground people don't understand is I'm doing this for *them.* Sure, most can't afford an Icarus. Hardly anyone, not one in a million. But Dad worked hard for these wings, even if he didn't know that's what his striving would buy. He wanted me to be happy, a happy failure. Maybe one day everybody will be able to afford an experience like this. Probably not but who knows? It all starts somewhere and for right now, those people – the angry woman the children the dogs the old man – can look up. They can see, they can *wonder* at what humans can accomplish. I'm their astronaut, a symbol of what can be achieved.

On the other side of town, I look for a good place to land. Dale warned me that the metro airfields are teeming with police, government inspectors, protesters. He's got my back, I should send him a bottle of wine.

I find a good spot in the middle of a dusty dry football field. I come back down to Earth, just the same as everyone else, and I phone my driver, tell him to come pick me up.

A House, Divided

hate your shower. That eco-friendly showerhead you bought with our money. The thin nozzle. It's one thing I don't miss at all.

It's dusk, and I'm making myself a toasted sandwich. It's what I eat almost every night, but I suppose you know that. My room – what used to be our living room – has a persistent stink of fried cheese, and the television cabinet is spattered with grease. What else can I do? You are in the kitchen, and I don't visit the kitchen while you're cooking.

The night you drew the border, I didn't argue. I was as sick of you as you were of me. You were slicing an avocado, and as usual you were doing it all wrong, even though I'd showed you many times how to keep the skin intact. When you looked around, something in my expression must have given me away.

What happened next occurred without words: by then we had spoken all the words. You put down the mangled avocado, and the knife, and left the room. Not knowing what to do, not wanting to do anything, I stood and watched a bead of moisture form on the underside of our tap. Convex, glinting, it couldn't quite muster the substance to break away and drop into the sink.

I could hear you moving things around in our closet. When you returned, you were carrying a brush and a tin of paint – the small one we kept to touch up walls, hide scrapes. You placed your hand on my chest and walked me backwards until I stood by the door to our living room. I gave no thought to resistance: I was curious, and tired of the fight.

I watched you streak a thick white line across the floor-boards. When you reached the table in the centre of the room, you raised the brush, paint flicking and dribbling. You kept the line going straight down the centre of the table, and the floor on the other side, and up the bench and along until the brush slapped the wall. When it was done, you spoke to me one last time. 'You,' you said, pointing to my side.

Every kingdom divided against itself is brought to desolation. But now we are two kings. Two kingdoms. The pope in the east and the pope in the west.

My domain:
* half a kitchen
* main bathroom and adjoining w.c.
* former living room; now a combined bedroom/office/lounge
* balcony (west-facing).

Your domain:
* half a kitchen
* study (small)
* master bedroom with ensuite
* laundry
* storage closet
* front door leading to stairwell.

At the time of the partition, nothing struck me as unfair. It seemed spontaneous, but now I wonder whether you planned it.

The way you split the kitchen meant that the sink, the fridge, the cooktop, and most of the useful appliances fell on your side. I retained the kettle and the pantry, and the shelf full of crockery we received for our engagement and never put to work. My toasted sandwiches are now served on bone china plates with a navy trim and gold banding – the stuffy ones we agreed never to bother with unless actual royalty came to visit. I wash up in the bathroom sink, plates drying in the bathtub. I take care not to let anything chip.

You got the front door, too, and it's hard to overstate how inconvenient that is. Our whole arrangement – peace without victory – would have been unworkable if it weren't for the balcony, and the fact that we're only one floor off the ground. I have a rope ladder that I lower and raise like I'm living in a fort. I've explained everything to our downstairs neighbours, Faisal and Natasha, so that they don't call the police when they see someone dangling next to their patio. I don't go into the history. It's never productive to delve into the history, but all the same, Faisal is generous with his commiserations. Natasha does her best to ignore me. So we've split them, too.

◆

Imagine being another person. Imagine inhabiting their body and their mind for six months, say, or twelve, and understanding what made them work – at least insofar as that person understood it themselves. With that kind of understanding must come forgiveness, each act capable of being related back to its inciting thoughts and emotions.

That's not how we work – by 'we' I could easily mean you and I, but really I mean we, humans. The justifications we offer are inadequate. That's a failure of language, sure, but mainly it's a failure of faith: faith in others, faith that if a perfect truth is offered up, perfect absolution will follow.

Even more than your body, I miss those rare, evanescent moments when you became knowable. You hesitated, once, in the act of pouring cereal into a bowl, trying to decide the best amount to eat, as if there was a single, objectively correct answer to such a complicated question. Another time, your expression changed in a particular way that I remember very clearly, but couldn't hope to describe, and you looked right past me, and even though we were talking about how to get grease stains out of denim, I knew you were remembering your mother.

◆

I made a winch. It helped me get the bar fridge up and over the railing. The fridge huddles next to my bed, keeping my dairy items cool, and it hums. At night, it reminds me of you. When we shared a bed and I came in late, you would sometimes make welcoming noises. *Mmm?* Rising in tone, questioning, approving. Other times, even as you continued to dream, I could tell I'd interrupted you. You grunted as I drew back the sheet. You were affronted by my presence, or my former absence, or both.

Love is leaning forward. You lean forward and out, and then one day, just for a moment, you forget. You relax, and rock back so that your weight rests on your heels. That's all it takes.

In the afternoons I hear you talking on the phone, your voice muffled through the wall. It's the closest thing I have to conversation, and I take comfort in your nearness. Some nights you don't come home at all. I know when that happens, because I am awake listening for the front door.

I'm not as lonely as you might imagine. Sometimes I feel like there's another person inside, watching through my eyes, a person who would make different choices if they could seize the machinery of my body. I'm not possessed, or hearing voices or anything. I suppose it's just my way of explaining a connection that runs through all of us, if we're receptive. In these last few months, I've had time and space.

This is how it needs to be. We are unreconciled. I could heave all my stuff off the balcony and find another place, but I can't bear the thought of another so near you, lying on this fold-out mattress. Or worse, and more realistically, sharing the bed you've claimed. And you must feel the same, you *must*, or why would you tolerate this? Every day is another chance for union. It wouldn't take much.

Some nights, when I am sure you must be asleep, I cross the border. The floorboards don't protest. I lap at water from the kitchen sink, rearrange the magnets on the fridge. I put the palm of my hand on your closed bedroom door. I breathe your air, and remember you, and the time when we shared it all.

Else / If

```php
<?php
/*This is a script to help me model your chances of dying.*/

/*Anything surrounded by slashes and stars – this, for example –
is a comment. It doesn't affect output. It's just here to remind
the programmer what she's doing. If you saw this script in
action – you never will – these comments would be hidden
from you.*/

/*You rest in the next room over, quarantined by gyprock and
wood. I should be working, debugging a legacy site for a client,
but instead I'm writing this dirty, rushed code, so far from best
practice it's not funny. But how else am I supposed to concen-
trate? I need to be prepared.*/

/*Define the base chance of dying of this illness, all other things
being equal:*/
$baseChance = 2.00;
echo <<<EOT
Your base chance of death, before relevant modifiers are applied,
is $baseChance%<p>
EOT;
```

/*A two per cent probability. You're negative for the pandemic-*du-jour*. We know that much, at least, since I badgered you into spending an afternoon queuing for a test. It's undoubtedly definitely almost certainly just the flu. You're in your prime, strong. But people do die from plain old influenza: a couple of thousand most years just in Australia. I must be overestimating the risk, but it's hard to get a reliable death rate for young infected adults in a developed country with no pre-existing conditions. I tried the CDC and the WHO and Wikipedia, but no luck.*/

$misdiagnosis = $_REQUEST['misDiag'];
/*This command retrieves a value from a web form that asks: was there a misdiagnosis of your condition? Maybe what's causing your fever is not a virus at all. I'll admit that I've been googling your symptoms. What if it's your kidneys shutting down, or your liver? When we went to the clinic, your doctor seemed distracted. It was just before her lunch break, and she didn't test you. She just said that *in all likelihood* what you have is run-of-the-mill, seasonal flu.*/

if ($misdiagnosis == true) {
        /*That is, if there was a misdiagnosis ...*/
        /*... then:*/
        $baseChance = 5.00;
        echo 'There was a mistake. You don't have influenza –
        you have something else. Chance of death now 5%<p>';
}

/*This is a blunt instrument, but no time to hone it. I need to take a break and check on you.*/

/*Is it our house? It's cold here in the winter, in the high hills, the paddocks white with frost in the mornings, the clouds brushing us. The birds struck dumb. Twenty minutes from the city's edge, but even so, we're isolated. The internet cuts out when it rains.*/

/*The cold gets in no matter how many hot-water bottles we hide between blankets. It rises from the slate floor. The fire, well stoked in our kitchen, hardly takes the edge off. Wood-smoke smell permeates the house. Maybe we'll smoke out your sickness, packing the rooms with carbon particulates like a priest swinging his censer.*/

/*Maybe we should call for a priest.*/

$wellCaredFor = $_REQUEST['wellCared'];
/*I will try to be attentive, but I might neglect you. I work and I visit the shops, and I spend too long trying to cook good broth. While you are laid up, I feed the chickens and check on the sheep. I might make a mistake and keep you too hot in your bed, stewing like a snail in an oven. I might give you water or food at the wrong times, in the wrong quantities. I might miss some important sign that marks a change.*/

/*I felt your forehead again. You stirred, told me *I love you*. You tend not to say it like that. You nod, or squeeze me, or mumble *You too* after I've made a declaration.*/

/*Why would you say it like that?*/

/*Your skin is slick. For anyone who has known you in health, your face is marked with suffering. It's there in the crease between your eyebrows and the bridge of your nose; the way your chin juts out a bit too far from your throat, your head tilted back. If you reached out your arm towards me, we could be art models for some Pre-Raphaelite deathbed scene.*/

/*The sour smell in here would make anyone think that you've been wrapped in our linen for twenty days straight, but it's only been two.*/

```
if ($wellCaredFor == true) {
        $baseChance = $baseChance * 0.8;
        echo 'I have done a good job caring for you, reducing
        your chances of dying by 20%<p>';
        /*Good on me.*/
```

/*You looked after me so well when I had my wisdom teeth out. You can be rough with the animals, so I was surprised. We'd only been seeing each other for a few months, but you stayed the whole weekend. You made me raspberry jelly and I ate strong painkillers and beat you at chess, four times.*/

/*I bled from my gums and considered you. I knew you were a good one. You would stick with me.*/

```
}
```

else {

/*If I cared poorly for you ... */
$baseChance = $baseChance * 1.5;
echo 'I have done a bad job caring for you, increasing your chances of dying by 50%<p>';

}

/*Off a low base. So if there was a 2% chance of you dying, now there is a 3% chance.*/

/*On your feet, you take up space. In our bed, too. You struck me as robust, and I won't pretend that wasn't part of your appeal. When we met, the idea that I could be with a farm boy was funny. It's still funny.*/

/*Of course, Mark was fit too, when I met him. I was studying, enjoying my twenties, not looking for anything permanent. But Mark was thirty-one, and persuasive. Six good years together and though he worked too hard, he never let himself go. When he collapsed on the treadmill I buried him and wept with his family. Afterwards, a report described an atrial septal defect, a hole in the heart. Subtle. Undiagnosed; Mark had never known. Still, it caused the stroke.*/

/*A good programmer makes provision for unlikely failure; the one-in-a-million. 'Exception handling', it's called. Mark taught me to keep the edge cases in mind.*/

/*I was sure I hadn't made another mistake. You are my Version Two, and you don't go to the gym. You lift hay bales and you walk with long strides. But now you're properly sick. It's the first time since I've known you. It's a betrayal.*/

$newStrain = $_REQUEST['newStrain'];
/*Back in 2009, a pandemic was caused by the A/H1N1/09 strain − swine flu, jumped across to humans. Children, especially, had no cross-reactive antibody response to the new strain. Before that it was SARS; afterwards, it was MERS; then came a new coronavirus, and by that time we were accustomed to grim acronyms. We have crowded every habitable part of the Earth, hungry for all forms of protein, and it's inevitable that new variants will emerge. Types that we've no resistance to. Types that kill quickly.*/

/*When you woke up this morning, I asked how you felt and you said, *A bit COVID-y.* I laughed, because of course your test came back negative, and I want you to think that I can take a joke, but really I don't think it's funny at all.*/

/*The night before your fever started, we had an argument. It was about everything – our house, the mortgage, my work, your work, my first husband, your chauvinist father. Children and the lack of them.*/

/*Afterwards, even though we couldn't look at each other, you made me instant ramen.*/

/*It's always a strain, of one type or another. You trod the paddocks in your gumboots, spending long days answering the demands of this place. Now your struggles are simpler: for lucidity, for healing. I shouldn't fight with you about dumb things.*/

```
if ($newStrain == true) {
        $baseChance = $baseChance * 3;
        echo 'What you've contracted is a virus. But it's not
        just-the-flu after all, it's something new. Your chance
        of dying has tripled.<p>';
}
```

/*I pay attention to the rhythms of my body, trying to establish a feedback loop. Seeking some trace – perhaps if I catch whatever you've got, I'll have more data points, be able to refine this script to make it more accurate. Or would it become less accurate, more subjective? Bodies can lie, like when I think I'm pregnant, but I'm not.*/

/*Humans are too complex to be efficient. Machines are easier. In the time I've sat here, worrying about you, some background process left running in my mind has identified the bad code screwing up this website I'm supposed to be working on. Before you wake up, it will have been corrected.*/

```
$hospitalised = $_REQUEST['hosp'];
```
/*If you get worse, or if you just don't get better, you might need to go to hospital. That would mean your condition is serious.

And as we all know by now, hospitals come with their own set of risks.*/

```
if ($hospitalised == true) {
        echo 'You have taken a turn for the worse. You have been
        admitted to hospital.<p>';
        $competentStaff = $_REQUEST['competent'];
        /*At least everyone's had a lot of practice recently.*/

        if ($competentStaff == true) {
            $baseChance = $baseChance * 0.8;
            echo 'The well-trained staff are attentive to your
            needs, reducing your chance of death by 20%<p>';
            /*This is the more likely scenario. The horror stories
            must be the exception, not the rule.*/
        }
        else {
            $baseChance = $baseChance * 1.5;
            echo 'Whether through overwork, crowding or
            lack of equipment, you receive sub-standard care
            in hospital. Your chance of death has increased by
            50%<p>';
        }
        /*What else might happen to you?*/

        $infection = $_REQUEST['infect'];
        /*While in hospital, with your immune system already
        weakened, you could develop a secondary infection, like
        secondary bacterial pneumonia.*/
```

```
    if ($infection == true) {
        $baseChance = $baseChance * 2;
        echo 'In hospital, you develop a secondary infection,
        doubling your chance of death.<p>';
    }
} /*End if ($hospitalised == true)*/


/*Time to tally everything up. If there's a god, perhaps she per-
forms a similar accounting.*/
echo <<<EOT
All factors considered, your chance of death is $baseChance%<p>
EOT;
echo 'Computing outcome now.<p>';


/*Generate a random number between 1 and 100. This is the
roll of the dice. If this random number exceeds the probabil-
ity score we've calculated – the $baseChance variable – that is
good news for you.*/
$randNum = rand (1,100);
if ($baseChance < $randNum){
        echo 'Congratulations! You survived!';
        /*Of course, this very simple program doesn't address
        quality-of-life issues. What will happen if your lungs
        are damaged? We couldn't stay on the farm.*/
}
else {
        echo 'You died.';
        /* ... */
}
```

/*I know this is irrational, this fear. Losing one partner does not affect the likelihood of losing another. I wrote this script to remind me of that, and I'll never tell you about it.*/

/*Every day of worry is a loop, and loops can be broken. I just need to find the right conditions, so I'll run this over and again. Usually, you live. Almost always. If I set this program running a thousand times, you'll survive more than nine hundred of those tests.*/

/*When you die, I will revive you; reset you. Bring you back. And on the next try, you will make it through.*/

/*You are on the other side of this wall. And when I go in to check, when I listen to you breathe, I know how fragile you are. The unfairness of a single iteration.*/

/*Please get well. Get well soon.*/
?>

The Mind–Body Problem

Day 1

A clamour of guards, detainees and locals met us at the dock. The only sounds on the boat had been the engine and the bruise of waves against hull, and I was not prepared. Even before the lines had been tied, men jumped aboard and started hoisting our cargo, while others undid the zips on our luggage, inspected contents, and conferred in their own languages.

I asked if it was permitted to use labour from the camp for this purpose, and one of the guards told me this group had volunteered. Before I could properly introduce myself, some of our smaller items were carried up a path towards the dark, green interior, bags and bearers lost from view. I sent Raul to follow. Our equipment is precious and must be accounted for.

Day 4

One way to study the mind–body problem is through deprivation, so we were pleased when the Department granted our request.

Now that we've acclimated, and I have set up my workspace just so, I am eager to begin. My colleagues feel the same: they are overfull of plans and pet hypotheses. From a research perspective, conditions are close to ideal. A multitude of UMAs in an isolated location, rights curtailed. Reporters and trouble-makers prohibited.

This place resembles a quarry. During the day, the oomahs (we've adopted the term from the security team) mill behind wire screens. Vegetation is kept well back from the main admin-istration building and the tents, exposing a straw-coloured loam that dominates the ground and the graded walls. Pale yellow below, unremitting blue above. Years ago, at a faculty party, a poet friend of mine described beauty as *the spirit finding nour-ishment in the real*, and I often recall those words when struck by something pleasing to the eye. But there is no sustenance here.

My team and the oomahs don't know what to make of each other. We attempt nervous smiles, and they respond with averted glances. The women keep their distance, and the chil-dren ignore us entirely, incurious about the presence of strangers. I tell them we are Australian, that we come from the place they were trying to reach. That should count for something, but I suppose it will take time to establish a rapport. A few of the guards have managed it; they saunter around the mess, stop-ping here and there to trade a few sentences. They return the soccer ball when it strays out of bounds. They put their hands on the shoulders of the oomahs or an arm around their necks in a manner that indicates familiarity.

A quarry, yes. And no shortage of raw material.

Day 9

Via satellite link, news of the controversy back home has reached us. How did our project get past the ethics committee? The truth is that with the amount of private funding on offer, the university was never going to knock this back. Politically, it was an easy sell: the arrivals, unwilling to return to their points of origin, subsist on taxpayer funds. Why shouldn't the taxpayer see a corresponding benefit? But compared to our work, the politics hardly matters.

As project lead, it falls to me to justify. Yesterday, a message from a journalist tripped the filter. I responded, on background, that our presence should be reassuring. We are here to observe. There will be a record of what is done.

Day 15

Where does the mind wander when the body is neglected? To investigate, Raul and his team of substance dualists are spending time with oomahs who refuse food. Might a wasting body expose the soul underneath? Raul assures me it's nothing as pseudo-scientific as that.

We avoid the ones who've sewn shut their lips; that's thought to indicate too much agency. Raul prefers those who lay on their cots, unwilling to move. While I would never tell him in so many words, I believe that he is committing a basic error. The substance dualism team are working backwards from their preferred theory, seeking to confirm it. I may be in the minority, but I have come here with an open mind.

In the camp proper, the heat is difficult to bear. For the most part, when not observing, we shelter in the demountable offices. Air conditioner. Dehumidifier. In such an alien place, these things help us persist.

Day 34

Every day is a new thought. The idealists – led ably by my ex-pupil, now colleague, Francis – have turned their attention to oomahs who claim to have been assaulted. At first, the security team were reluctant to describe their methods. But now that the local government has conferred immunity for all past acts, the guards are more forthcoming. Many of them have been here for twelve months or more. They have compiled a litany of grievances, and they appreciate having a new audience. Though the guards themselves are not the subject of study, their candour has been useful as we attempt to document cause and effect.

Idealists hold that matter is an illusion, flesh and bone a construct of pure thought. But the abused subjects reject this interpretation in the strongest terms. So far, this line of enquiry has failed to bear fruit.

Day 46

Nothing is more fundamental to our humanity than finding an answer to the mind–body problem. Where, precisely, is our consciousness located? In the borderlands of science, philosophy and religion, too many areas remain uncharted. I firmly believe that answers exist, and once we find them, we will be capable of understanding.

Today an older subject approached me when I entered the main compound. He has dark, scruffy hair and a ready smile. As far as I can tell, the rest of his people defer to him. I looked him up: he has been here for more than a decade, which speaks of fortitude. The guards call him Billy, a simplification of the name he arrived with.

Billy told me how happy he is to be able to assist us. I understood him perfectly: after being cast out, or forced to flee one's home, our project must be a comfort. Before we arrived, the oomahs were bereft of any purpose.

After we had talked for a while, he asked me for a cigarette. I told him I don't smoke.

Day 51

Most frustrating day. Zero progress towards my own research goals.

One of the PhD candidates was caught recording an interview session on her phone. She was isolated immediately and, under questioning, admitted to a loss of objectivity. She was planning to smuggle footage out, to draw attention to the 'plight' (her word) of the oomahs.

She will be sent home tomorrow. Her association with the university will end, and of course she will be reminded about her confidentiality obligations, and potential civil and criminal repercussions of any breach. It would be destructive and self-aggrandising, but I suppose she will want to *tell her story*. All the more reason to re-commit ourselves to our work, since our time here may be short.

Francis is mortified – she was the offender's supervisor. This afternoon we spoke at length in my office. I am confident that Francis had no prior knowledge of the misconduct, and that she continues to believe in the critical importance of our project. Putting aside the difficult circumstances, I admire her commitment. We have agreed to check in more frequently.

Day 76

The room I sleep in is starting to feel like— Not like home. But the space feels worn in. I can find the light switch in the dark, and my feet know the number of steps to the wash basin.

Some of the oomahs participate in craft activities between studies (you see: we afford latitude where we can, where this does not conflict with our work plan). They have been braiding strips torn from old bedsheets, coloured with food dye lifted from the storeroom by one of the more sympathetic guards. I took an example of their efforts and, with cable ties and industrial staples, attached it to the wall opposite my mattress. It mitigates the plastic and the corrugated metal.

In the camp, the dust is unavoidable. It sticks to skin, hair and clothing. I carry it around, contaminate the surfaces. My chair, and my desk. I sweep often, to little effect.

Day 80

Now that I know his face, and he knows who I am, I seem to run into Billy all the time. He asks if I am well, and I tell him, yes, I am very well. He pesters me about his family, and patiently I explain that I don't have the information he wants, and have no means of getting it. Billy takes this in his stride, and I respect his equanimity.

Billy was a high-school teacher. If I let him, he would tell me how he came here, and why he believes he can't return to his homeland. But that isn't germane to our research, and for the most part I discourage talk about the oomahs' failed or pending claims. If his story is a sham, I don't want to know. And if it became apparent that he truly had been persecuted – that knowledge would complicate our interactions.

If he is ever resettled, he says he will be happy to do any kind of work. Perhaps cooking in a kitchen, or labouring. He doesn't care where he lives, but he would like to raise a few citrus trees.

Billy has a quality, a value, that is uncommon. There must be a way to better utilise him.

Day 94

Our island is small, but even so, it is possible to find places to be alone.

Some days, nothing changes from the day before. The camp is still. There is no traffic in the sky, and it becomes difficult to remember our mission. On those cloudless days I want to lie on my bed like an oomah and wait for the time to pass. Instead, I walk until I find a beach, and study the garbage on the sand. Bags. Containers for fried chicken, ripped and empty. How did they make it so far? All scraps of plastic have an origin, which I try to guess at, and it reminds me that we are connected. What we do here will wash back out.

Day 113

Several of our cohort have become interested in the five-aggregate model, which holds that the mind is a mystical grab-bag of sense impressions and phenomena. Perhaps I am over-simplifying. In any case, they requisitioned a group of fifteen child-oomahs for specialised analysis, calling for isolation and privacy. I have my doubts about the value of this effort, but Raul vouched for the team leader, who was also commended to me by our project's benefactor. Out of professional respect, I helped make the arrangements.

Due to its greater plasticity, a juvenile brain may facilitate easier study of the mind-stream as stimuli are applied and then removed. The experience of past and recent trauma is a confounding factor, but one that can be partially controlled for. Efforts continue.

Day 115

Today, Billy lost his foot.

Hookworms endemic to this place had taken root in his left heel, resulting in creeping eruption. Billy complained, but his situation was judged non-critical. Days later, when the site was re-examined, abrasions from scratching had led to sepsis too entrenched to treat with antibiotics. I made my displeasure known to the medic, but she rattled off the usual complaints about caseload.

An amputation was scheduled for the early afternoon. I was invited in case any useful data might be gleaned, but I made an excuse. I confess, the idea of watching Billy's foot part from his still-living body revolted me. Does that make me weak? Does that matter? Others were able to do what was necessary.

Afterwards, I visited. Billy was awake, and silent. Analgesics dulled his eyes, but could not mask his grief. What exactly did he mourn? I watched him and thought about wounds that are both physical and spiritual.

I told him that I had been investigating token identity physicalism, which holds that mental states need not have fixed biological correlates. One person's discomfort may be another's agony, and that meant that the pain he felt was *his* pain, to do with as he pleased. I meant this kindly, but Billy wouldn't lift his gaze from the bedsheet.

Day 121

I have become close with Francis.

After our work is done, she visits my quarters. We drink white rum and rub each other with ice cubes cultivated in my bar fridge. Rank has its privileges.

Today I kept still and watched closely as Francis slid ice upwards from my kneecap along my thigh. Meltwater spilled down in trickles, forming droplets on the fine hairs. My hair. *My* hair. There's something in that.

Day 134

This speculation about the five-aggregate study is making everyone restless. The guards, who usually prefer to leave well enough alone, mutter and fall quiet when I enter the staff kitchen.

Perhaps there is too much fraternisation with the oomahs? Sometimes I think they know more than I do. How do I reassure them?

I'll have a word with Raul next time I see him, but he's started sleeping at B Facility, on the other side of the island. In a rambling email last week, he wrote (again, again) that matters are reaching a critical point.

Day 152

Last night I dreamed that we were shooting men out of cannons, towards Mars. To shield them against the cold of outer space, we slathered each human projectile in a paste of lead and cadmium. We were trying to keep them safe, but by the time they reached their destination they were so poisoned that all they could do was lie in the dust and look at a strange sky.

No person on this island sets out to cause misery. But misery is natural, and where it occurs, we have a duty to witness. The implications of our research are becoming clearer now, not least for those we experiment upon. For ourselves. But if we don't act with rigour, and follow leads to their conclusion, our results could be worse than useless. We owe it to the oomahs to see this through.

Day 177

Given what has occurred, I will choose my words carefully.

After the failure of the five-aggregate study, several of the subjects were returned to the main camp. Some had been damaged. The parents of these – and the parents of the oomahs that were not returned – became agitated, and this was the proximate cause of the rioting.

I cannot overstate the harm this incident has done to our research efforts. Several of our most interesting subjects were lost in the fighting. Our main examination facility has been partly destroyed.

I fielded a tense call from the minister's chief of staff. I assured him in the strongest possible terms that the situation was now under control and that the recalcitrant oomahs have been subdued. He said that one such incident may be forgivable, but there could be no recurrence.

As internal sponsor of the study, Raul has taken full responsibility for the affair and has departed. No great loss, since his own research had stagnated. Meanwhile, I have ordered a tightening of movement about the camp, and split the population into manageable sub-groups.

Day 190

I was the one who found Billy, as he must have intended.

Following his injury, he had adopted silence and a passive affect. Given his limited mobility, he was deemed non-threatening and granted a measure of freedom to make his way as best he could about the camp. We will continue to investigate how he obtained the knife, but no doubt the answer will be unsatisfying. Disregard of security protocols. Malaise. A long-ago broken lock that no-one thought to repair.

I had been working with Billy personally since the amputation. Willingly or otherwise, he was helping me to understand something.

Day 243

After taking part in this effort and observing the oomahs for several months, I now believe that if our consciousness – our soul – resides anywhere, it is diffused within our physical forms. We are not merely shaped by our experiences. At an essential level, who we are depends on how our bodies are treated.

God help me. If they tow a few more vessels our way, I think I can prove it.

The Lever, the Pulley and the Screw

Leon: is moving heaven and earth. Asks only for a place to stand. Stands on the second floor, in his fishbowl office with its view of the open plan, three levels down from Executive. Has been tasked with project completion, on time and on budget. Must find a way to deliver. Will get his bonus. In view of resource constraints, the only path forward is to exert small force in hope of large effect.

Paula: is ideal efficiency. Power in equals power out. Supports movement. Supports frequent changes of direction. Lifts others up, even as they kick and scream. Keeps her hair above her collar and the calendar up to date. Misses her friends. Transmits tension.

Scott: is a simple machine. Amplifies force. Knows his place, and Paula's. Does same job, but he's paid 10k more so there's the pecking order. Wears a tie, even on casual Fridays. Uses his body to block the exit. Revels in friction. Has a beard, but not the right kind of beard. Can work a fax machine; struggles with video-conferencing. Slides along his axis, forcing himself further. Self-locking. Try as the bastards might, they'll never work him loose.

Leon: understands what this company is about. It's about engineering and creation. Or it will be, one day soon. Right now, they need to convince enough investors that the Outer-Metro Underground Tollway is a good idea. Maybe not necessary, maybe not practical, but lucrative. His business card announces him as Head of Investor Relations, and the head is where the brain lives. He updates shareholders about lobbying efforts, regulatory approvals, environmental impact statements, resident consultations, cost overruns, time overruns (within expected contingencies), the next round of capital raising. Leon and his small team are preparing an offer document. It's time-critical. Must be persuasive, must be accurate. No pressure.

Paula: knows that Leon appreciates her, even if he doesn't say it. Has her hand on a thick pile of reports. Has her period, and an ache at the base of her spine that is probably related, but which she hasn't felt before and wonders if she should see a doctor about.

Scott: sits at his desk, tending to management aspirations. Sips black coffee from the machine in the staff kitchen. Prefers his coffee white, but no-one ever flushes the tube between the milk jug and the frother, so the milk comes out chunky. Compensates with two heaped teaspoons of sugar, but it can't hide the scorched taste of the beans. Will go on holiday to Noosa when this is all over. Will drink piña coladas, like in the song. Until then, holds it together, vice-like.

Leon: knows that there's an art to delegation. The pyramids were built with a gesture, it was written in a book he purchased at the airport. Is wearing his pink shirt, French cuffs. Is terrified that Paula will walk. Needs her too much to ever thank her. It's hard to find good help. What's needed now is a quiet word with Scott, a warning in his tone.

Paula: writes the reports, emails the stakeholders, mediates the fights, absorbs the aggro, works late nights, works weekends, ignores the pay freeze.

Scott: is old enough to remember when roads and tunnels were built by the government.

Leon: has a life, you know. Outside of work. Has a studio. Makes electroclash when he can get a moment away from wife and baby. Last night, spent four hours trying to get a drum loop just right. He can tell it's not there yet, but he doesn't understand why. He's trawled through the sample libraries. It's not the rhythmic phrasing, or the variety of the sonic palette, or the closed hi-hat, or the pitch of the snare. Why doesn't it sound like the tracks they play on the radio?

Paula: believes, despite all evidence, that hard work will be rewarded.

Scott: is on his sofa at home, watching the football, slouched for maximum comfort, hands resting on paunch. It is eight-thirty pm on a Thursday night. Has a beer on the side table and a cold in his sinuses. His team, the Trilobites, are losing what should be a very winnable match against the Giraffes. When it's over, he will turn the TV off, put all the empty cans next to the back door, remove his clothes and climb into bed. He will dream that he is being rocked to sleep in the arms of a giant woman, taller than the hills, his head nestled between the crook of her arm and her breast.

Leon: bleeds perspiration onto the edges of an A3 spreadsheet. The columns represent the days, and each row is a task. Most boxes are pale green, but his computer has charted progress against plan, and helpfully re-shaded some of the boxes red.

Paula: wakes up, realises it's Monday. Thinks about calling in sick, pushes the thought away. But then she reconsiders, works it through, and OMG she actually does it. Knows that this is so unprecedented, Leon won't ask for a doctor's note.

Scott: is in a conference with a young girl from Legal. He's doing his level best to stay calm, he really is, as he explains how they've derived an input to the financial projections. But the girl just keeps saying that it's not sound, and referencing the Corps Act as if Scott ought to know the section by heart. And it's one of those conversations where she's not listening to what he's saying, and he hasn't got the faintest idea what she's saying, and they are already writing emails to their managers in their heads, escalating the dispute.

Leon, Paula, Scott: are at the company's mid-year ball, down the end of a table that runs the length of the function room. The lights are low and it's hard to hear anything over smooth rock and chatter. Leon is miffed at the seating chart but doing his best not to show it. Paula is wishing she'd worn a different dress. Scott has bet Leon that he can drop a mini dim sim into the Operations Manager's glass of red wine without him noticing. And then OMG Scott actually does it. He wanders over to his target, claps him on the back, and points out something on the other side of the room. His other hand is already creeping, depositing the payload. Scott excuses himself and returns to Leon and Paula, both of whom applaud. The fact of an uncomplicated win is just so un-Scott-like that it must be congratulated. Paula makes a joke about MSG in the GSM, which Leon and Scott don't get, but it doesn't matter. For a little while they feel like comrades.

Scott: wakes up the next day. Groggy, but without the usual angry/sad sense of panic that the weekend has started to burn.

Paula: wonders why they always talk about building, not digging. How can you build a hole?

Leon: is browsing Facebook on his computer, screen angled away from the glass wall, wishing he could concentrate on the traffic-flow modelling report he knows he should be reading, and wondering whether someone in IT monitors his browsing history.

Scott: thinks often about getting a dog, but can't do it. It'd be waiting while Scott was at work, shut up in his courtyard. No creature should spend that much time alone.

Paula: is being interrogated by her niece, who is asking whether Paula will have a baby soon. They are playing snakes and ladders, and the question is unexpected, and it takes Paula a few seconds before she says probably not, probably not soon. The girl says oh, but in a little while you will get too old. This seems like an unusual thing for a six-year-old to know. It must have come down from the girl's mother, Paula's sister-in-law, and Paula thinks, thank you very much, you instagramming, kale-masticating, hot-yoga-sweating, 0.4 FTE renaissance woman.

Leon: is a betting man. And he bets they will never build this tunnel. Glances again at the crease-worn spreadsheet, traces the critical path with his finger, swearing fuck fuck fuck.

Scott: could really use a fuck. But not Paula; you don't shit where you eat. And the girls in HR are up themselves. Since his divorce he's started going to the pub with a couple of mates on a Friday night but he never gets any action.

Paula: could really use a fuck. But the men in the office make her queasy. There are too many of them, they are too close.

Leon: wonders when his lunch will get delivered.

Scott: is shouting at Paula, is threatening her because of a word. He has written that *the initial soil testing is complete.* In a marked-up document sent back and copied to Leon, Paula has inserted the word *substantially* after the word *is.* She explains that she has done this because the soil testing is not complete, not entirely, but to Scott it's clear she's trying to sabotage him. He screams at her to get back in her box, that if he wants her opinion he'll bloody well ask for it. Two cubes over, Jordan from Accounts Payable raises his head to see what's going on.

Paula: knows better than to listen to Scott. Takes the stairs, finds herself outside, blinking back tears. It's freezing and that helps. She walks fast, habit delivering her to a nearby mall, and down into the basement of a food court where she purchases a blueberry muffin and a bottle of water, and wishes she'd thought to bring earbuds so she could drown out the attack of conversation bouncing off the tiled floor and the stainless-steel walls.

Leon: wants to tell Paula not to dress like an old maid. Wants to tell Scott that it's never going to happen for him, he's just not made of the right components. But he has to keep all that to himself, jolly them along, ration the carrots. People are the hardest part of any job. People, when you get down to it, are really exhausting.

Scott: wakes at night, sick with fear and want.

Paula: wakes at night, editing a private task list.

Leon: wakes at night, wondering if he's been set up to fail.

Scott: half-listens to a webinar pushed out to all staff by the CIO, in which some management consultant is trying to use Fukushima as a parable about organisational responsiveness. But most of Scott is browsing online job listings. There are a couple of analyst positions going at the big accounting firms. The pay would be better, but at those places you've got to record your time. Who wants to justify their life, increment by increment? Better to stick it out here. There'll be recognition if this funding round ends up fully subscribed, Leon has basically promised as much.

Paula: catches sight of Leon at the outlet mall where she sometimes buys bed linen. It's Sunday, and he is sitting on a bench eating a sausage roll. Next to him is a woman with a pram. He wears shorts and boat shoes, and this is all wrong. She freezes, wondering if she should say hi. She thinks not. She turns and walks in the other direction, hoping he doesn't spot her.

Leon: wants to stop off at a pub on the way home, smack a fifty-dollar note down on the counter, and sink beers quietly, over hours, like his dad did back in the day. But there's no room for that. Time is something he owes to his employer, his family, his music. Time is not for him to fritter away.

Scott, Paula, Leon: all sense it. He, she, he, they know the absence at the centre of things, isolated under eggshell-thin concrete, masked by clanking shovels and thrown dirt.

Leon: is just about at the end of his rope, trying to keep everyone on task. It's the final week, they are nearing the very edge of the spreadsheet, beyond which the territory is unstructured. A final push, and they can do it. Late at night he buys them all pizza like the good boss he is, puts it on his own credit card. Can try and claim it back later but probably won't bother, you need to keep the receipts and the expense form is a pain in the arse.

Paula: doesn't mind the work, not really. It would be alright if all she had to do was her job. Derives quiet enjoyment from it when she's in the flow and checking off items and things are moving towards an end. Rides home on the train some days, looking at her fellow passengers, thinking, it could be worse, it could be worse.

Scott: is busting his balls. Makes sure Leon knows it, too, by sending him emails late at night, early in the morning. Makes a note every time Paula leaves the office before he does.

Leon: proofreads.

Paula: frowns.

Scott: lays his head on the desk.

Leon: has worked his team to breaking, worked himself to breaking, and OMG, actually got this done. Has vetted the copy, held the hands of the bosses through the verification, got sign-off from the board, and sent the final PDF to the printers in time for mail-out. Is summoned to level five, bloated with expectation, wiping his hands on the seat of his trousers. Gets a nod from the COO. Gets told – is reminded – there's a quarterly update due in three weeks, so this is no time to take his foot off the accelerator.

Paula: wants to tell Leon where to go. She can tell he thinks he's being magnanimous, giving her the afternoon off before they crack on with the next thing. But it's been weeks of hard slog. He tells her to go get a massage, a haircut. And she actually does want both of those things.

Scott: is waiting. For the email. For the call. Something good. Something bad. Something in him twists a quarter turn.

Leon, Paula, Scott: wear holes in each other, and one day they'll become unfit for purpose. For now, Leon can report: they are getting the job done.

No Good Deed

The first time, what brought Leah back was the crunch of gravel as her husband's ute pulled into the driveway. It must have been late, and when she tried to peer out the kitchen window, all she could see was her own reflection. From below, the sink issued a gurgle as washing-up water voided down the plughole. Her fingers, stuck fast in rubber gloves, felt damp and warm. In one hand she held a scourer and from the other, a baking tray dangled, dripping suds onto the floor. A carrot cake sat cooling on the granite benchtop.

Donny – still handsome even with his greying hair, always terrible at reading a room – came barrelling in, dropping his work boots by the door. 'What's this?' He made a show of sniffing the air. 'What have you done with my wife?' He stood behind her, leaning in to kiss her cheek.

Leah shrugged him off, started to peel away her gloves. This was all wrong. Amateur baking was a waste of time and materials, and the washing up was the cleaner's job. Donny seemed to like the cake, even though it was dry. But Leah couldn't remember how it had come into being. Not the mixing, or the pouring into the pan, or even the ingredients – had she used two eggs or three? The icing tasted like cream cheese and, yes, there was a half-used tub in the fridge. But what recipe had she followed?

The second episode happened on a Sunday afternoon. One minute she was sitting by the side of her tennis court, drinking pinot gris with her friends— . . . and then there was a gap. Without preamble, she found herself on her hands and knees in a muddy creek bed. Up on the bank, she saw a pile of bottles, chip packets and other detritus that might have been pulled from the long grass on either side of where she'd been crawling. Leah's favourite blue silk dress was ruined.

Her best friend explained later that Leah had bolted halfway through their get-together, wearing an idiot smile, completely unresponsive to questions. Everyone had thought it was a joke until Leah slammed her car door and reversed down the driveway. Courtside, her friends tutted indignantly as they finished off the wine. When school pick-up time rolled around and Leah still hadn't returned, they let themselves out.

The third time, Leah gave fifteen thousand dollars to charity. She gathered, based on the receipt she found later in her email inbox, that her donation would help animals whose homes had been destroyed by bushfire. Even now, hills were burning in another state.

'It's intolerable.' Leah squirmed, messing up the neat arrangement of the quilt. She was lying face-up on their super king, head resting on Donny's thick leg. He sat with his back against the headboard, leaning over her, massaging her scalp, getting in under her short brown hair with his fingers. Leah ignored his puzzled stare, fixing instead on a grey mark she'd noticed on the ceiling that would have to be painted over.

She often spoke of things he didn't fully comprehend, like when she railed about over-zealous conservation laws, or the latest bout of office politics. Even by those standards, her recent behaviour must have seemed baffling. Still, his fingers kept pressing above and behind her ears.

'What if next time, I end up donating to a bunch of activists?' she grumbled. 'If word got out, I'd be stuffed.'

Leah co-owned a firm of consulting archaeologists. That's what her business card said and that was how she introduced herself, but what it really meant was that she worked for a handful of big miners. To get a permit to dig or blast anywhere in the state, it was first necessary to consult with the traditional owners of the land. And before that came ethnographic and archaeological surveys that, from the miners' perspective, would ideally turn up little of significance. A heritage management plan would be prepared, with proposals for impact mitigation. Artefacts could be safely removed, and perhaps returned one day. Photographs and charts would memorialise the layout of the site before any ground disturbance. Sub-surface clearances would, probably, identify anything of interest that had not previously been noticed. And local land councils could appoint field officers to observe and assist (but not obstruct). Funds would be set aside to teach local children what had been there before the mine, and attitudinal surveys would confirm support for the company's plans.

Leah's team could help with all these things. It was lucrative work, and Leah had a formidable record. Of the nineteen projects she'd assessed during her career, none had stalled on heritage grounds. To some in her profession, that kind of record would have marked Leah as a sell-out. But her clients loved her, and Leah didn't mind when a friend or acquaintance questioned her ethics.

She'd got into this line of work because she'd wanted to be in the field, not stuck at a desk in some museum storeroom, cataloguing what had been found or appropriated by others. For the first decade or so, it had been exactly what she'd hoped it would be. Back then she was away more often than not, racking up hours in a double swag she'd customised for comfort. She loved looking up at the stars on a clear night, but when it was cold there was nothing better than zipping up, shutting the world out, and letting the air get funky. Archaeologists were oddballs, as a rule, but camp life was usually enjoyable. Most evenings the crew would drink themselves silly, and during the day they gave Leah plenty of space to think her own thoughts.

Promotions had followed, and then a stake in the business. Now it was difficult to escape the office for more than a couple of days at a time. She still loved the country, and she knew that a big find produced its own unstoppable momentum. Better to extract responsibly, with guidance from experts like her. Her projects were win-win situations, even if not absolutely everyone saw it like that.

◆

'I think it's wonderful,' Ruth said when she heard about Leah's fits of generosity. As she did every year on the seventh of the seventh, Leah had called the old chook. Between birthdays, Christmases, and updates when distant relatives kicked the bucket, they spoke every few months.

'You're finally giving back,' Ruth said. 'God is working through you, helping you to atone.'

Leah's mum still ran the chicken shop in the town where Leah had grown up. Ruth never had much money. The next town over had one of those big franchise restaurants peddling the Recipe, and it was hard to compete. Ruth had done a solid job for a single parent, but she was always trying to intervene, bestowing advice too eagerly and too often – not least on questions of morality. As far back as Leah could remember, she had felt stifled living in the granny flat behind the take-away. Decades later, the smell of chip grease still made her feel claustrophobic.

'I don't want to atone,' Leah said. 'I just want to stop these . . . episodes, attacks, whatever they are.'

'Go to a doctor, then. Better yet, talk to a priest.'

The following morning, Leah was late for work. She'd found herself on the side of the road, waving enthusiastically at a vehicle as it sped away. At her feet were the lug wrench and jack she usually kept in the well of her boot. Checking her car, she found that the spare tyre was missing.

She recognised the feeling now, when it was about to happen. Her chest would get hot, and she could smell something like dried basil, but sharper. Then, an absence, a lack, until she came back to herself moments or hours later.

As soon as she could get a referral, Leah described all of this to a neurologist. 'Interesting,' he said. 'Yes, very interesting. Could be a non-epileptic seizure, which would explain the memory loss and perhaps the smell. But the behaviour points to a kind of dissociative fugue.' He mentioned a conference he'd been to recently, which had been held on a cruise ship, and some papers he'd read which seemed to be of doubtful relevance. Leah wasn't following as closely as she might have. She kept getting distracted by the way the beams from the surgery's downlights scattered off the doctor's bald head. Leah let him prattle for another few minutes, wondering if she'd be billed for an extended consultation, before pointedly checking the time on her wristwatch.

She underwent a succession of tests. When the initial results showed no obvious cause, the neurologist said, 'Really, what we need is to look inside your head during one of these events.'

'I told you, they're random. I can't bring one on.'

The doctor leaned back in his chair and crossed one leg over the other. 'That does make things difficult.' He offered a weak, perfunctory smile.

Over the course of her career, Leah had wheedled, pestered and threatened – whatever it took – to keep her clients' projects on schedule. The most officious bureaucrats could not faze her. Nor could the laziest survey assistants, or the most self-righteous conservationists. By comparison, this duffer could surely be made to do his job. 'Here's how we'll play this,' she said. 'You'll put me in a hospital bed. Tie me down if you have to, so I don't do a runner. When it looks like I'm having an episode, pop me in the scanning machine.'

'The MRI. I'm afraid those machines are busy. You can't just . . . without a pre-booked window . . .'

'You'll do whatever it takes. No expense spared.' From the way he stiffened, his chin receding into the flesh of his neck, Leah wondered if she might have gone too far. 'I'm not myself when these things happen. What if I run out into traffic next time, cause a pile-up? Do you want that on your conscience?'

The doctor's mouth puckered and he huffed air out of full cheeks, like a football player who'd just blown a shot at goal.

'Besides ... I said no expense spared. Once we work this out, you'll tell me how I can show my gratitude. A charitable foundation, maybe, with you as chair, to help other poor bastards like me. Some of my clients run generous giving programs. Corporate social responsibility is what they call it now, they can't hand money out fast enough once they find the right story. I bet there's some new equipment you could use at your rooms. Or at the hospital ...' Leah had no idea how much *that* would cost, or if it was achievable. But that was a problem for another time.

She was admitted for observation, and suffered her next attack the following afternoon. When she regained awareness, Leah found herself in a hospital bed, the neurologist by her side. He displayed the kind of genuine affection that one hardly ever sees on the face of a busy practitioner.

'You get it done?'

The doctor nodded. 'You were in there for almost an hour. Very compliant. We were able to do some detailed mapping.'

'And what did you find?'

'Nothing significant. No tumours, no swelling. You're the owner of a healthy brain. But I would say ...' The doctor hesitated. 'I – we – myself and the MRI techs, we feel like we understand you better.

'I needed to get you talking,' he continued, when it was obvious she didn't remember. 'So that we could watch your language centres. I asked you for a joke, or a memory, and you said that you knew something about gratitude, because of what happened when you were a child. Things you only learned about much later.'

Leah felt herself tense. Her eyes wandered over the spotless floor.

'It must have been a lonely time for you. For your mother. You said I should remind you to visit her.'

Leah raised herself up, swung her legs so they dangled over the side of the bed, unfussed about the way the hospital gown rode up and bunched around her waist. She spoke slowly and deliberately, as if to a backward child. 'I couldn't give a rat's arse about any of that. Just tell me what's wrong with me.'

The warmth in the doctor's expression guttered out. 'Physiologically, I can't find anything wrong.' Because he was a professional, he refrained from any further assessment.

◆

Leah took a leave of absence from work. She didn't have a choice. What if she arrived one day and told the unvarnished truth? She might delete the last line she'd written in her current draft report – *Community perspectives about the project are mixed* – and fall to transcribing what she'd heard at the last consultation:

I learned the ways of my people from my older brothers. We are custodians, protecting our water, animals and totems as best we can. If this mine proceeds, it will devastate our land. It will disappear the place where our ancestors lived. These effects are irreversible, so we do not consent to this project. We do not consent.

Her field team had been shown engravings. In all probability, hundreds upon hundreds of generations had visited them, preserved them. Supplemented and renewed them. All those activities furthered the union of story and place, and the descendants of those creators had kept knowledge alive through the violence and erasure of the last two centuries. To carry away what had endured for so long, ostensibly in the name of preservation but really just to get at what was underneath, would be to inflict a new wound.

In one of her fits, Leah might openly criticise the system itself. How could it be that Leah, a consultant with no personal link to the site of the proposed mine, was considered more authoritative on this matter than the traditional owners? Their claims would only be given weight if supported by a blow-in like her. The process was so contaminated that no true understanding could ever result from it.

It was hard enough to hold these ideas in her mind, after years of avoidance. Leah knew that writing them down would be ruinous, professionally and personally, and she feared what she would do during her next absence.

◆

If there was nothing physically wrong with her brain, Leah reasoned, then she must be going mad. She held a deep distrust of anyone who sat around all day talking about feelings. But soon, after she caught herself giving a frail old woman a ride to the shops (a trace of mothballs and incontinence still lingered in her BMW), Leah gritted her teeth, made a few enquiries, and booked an appointment.

When Leah explained her situation, the psychologist smoothed her skirt and grasped for her notebook. 'Interesting,' she said.

They spoke for forty minutes, and Leah strove not to let her impatience show. They talked about her preschool years, when Leah's father was still on the scene. Her body image. Adolesence, isolation, and the complicated nature of mother-daughter bonds. It was exactly the sort of idiotic prying Leah had anticipated, but, as she explained, that stuff was irrelevant. She had moved on, geographically and emotionally, from the past. And Leah was happy with the way she looked. A solidly constructed woman, taller than most men, Leah enjoyed the presence that afforded her when she walked into a room. Most of the time she felt like a boss, and that made sense, because she was one. She didn't care about winning any beauty contests; she had a husband already and wasn't looking to trade him in. She almost never wore make-up. No, she had never wanted children of her own.

The psychologist, who was slight, had porcelain skin, and spoke very quietly, made a sort of humming noise when she'd run out of questions. She said, 'I don't suppose you're familiar with the work of Carl Jung?'

'No.'

'Jung believed that in everybody's unconscious, there is a part – he called it a person's 'shadow' – comprising the qualities that the conscious self has disowned. The qualities that are excluded when we describe ourselves to ourselves.' The psychologist leaned forward, placing her pen so that it rested in perfect orientation with the ruled lines of her notebook. 'But no-one is absolutely one thing or another, and so the more we deny the existence of our shadow, the more it manifests in unhelpful ways.'

Leah tugged at the cushion behind her back. 'Tripe. Pseudo-science.'

'You seem very self-reliant.'

This was hardly a searing insight, and Leah let out a sharp laugh. She thought about Donny, how they'd met when she was studying. Back then she'd worked shifts at a late-night grocery to support herself. Her husband was a good man, but his landscape gardening business had only ever brought in middling returns, barely contributing to their combined net worth.

'Independence, self-reliance,' the psychologist continued. 'Those are strengths. But independent people can be harsh, even cruel. Is that how you think about yourself?'

Leah smirked. 'You tell me.'

'I think you've been repressing your shadow – in your case, your generous, selfless tendencies – for so long that your unconscious is causing these episodes, as an outlet.

'What I'm telling you, Leah, is that if you want these attacks to stop, you should try embracing your shadow. Be kind. Do something kind for someone, consciously, because you choose to.'

Leah got to her feet. 'You better hope I'm feeling kind when I get your bill.' She started for the door.

In a hurried, breathy voice, the psychologist called after her. 'You're fascinating, you know. I wonder if you'd let me use you as a case study? I could talk about you at conferences. You'd just need to sign a consent form.'

'Over my dead body.'

'Well, keep it in mind.' The psychologist's mouth stayed botox-straight, but there was a troubling liveliness in her eyes. 'If your attacks don't stop, perhaps you'll reconsider.'

◆

Leah tried to forget all the rubbish she'd heard about shadows and repression, but then she suffered three more attacks in the space of a week. Valuable objects started to go missing from the house. Once, she came to her senses just in time to hear a metallic *thunnnng* as the flap closed on a charity donation bin. Try as she might, her arm wouldn't reach far enough down the chute to reclaim what she'd given. She didn't know what she'd dropped inside. But she felt a loss all the same.

Going against her strongest instincts, Leah made preparations to transfer her assets – the house, her superannuation fund, her share portfolio – into a protective trust. She read about powers of attorney and guardianship, and fretted about who she'd put in charge, if it came to that. Donny was honest but stupid; her usual lawyer perhaps too cunning.

The following Saturday, very early in the morning, she shook her husband to wake him. Donny snuffled in his sleep and tried to roll away. She whacked him hard on the meaty bit of flesh above his hip, leaving a red mark.

He'd been manhandled out the door and into the car before he received an explanation. 'We've got a round of golf booked at ten,' she said curtly. 'At that place down the coast, the one you've been rabbiting on about.'

'You hate golf.'

'I'll drive the buggy.'

Donny frowned. 'Are you having one of your . . . spells?'

Leah ignored him and turned out onto the road.

She spent the day spotting for her husband as he zig-zagged

up the fairways. She knew he was enjoying himself by the way he moved: unhurriedly and with loping strides, looking up at the sky and the trees.

They stopped in for a drink at the clubhouse when he'd finished. They sat side by side at the edge of a balcony overlooking the first tee, and took turns critiquing the form of the golfers starting their rounds.

'Do you think I'm a selfish person?' she asked.

He put down his beer. It took him a while to respond. 'How could I think that? Everything you have, you've shared with me.'

She let him pick the music on the drive home.

When she could stand it, she kept trying to be good. She called Ruth, just to talk. She volunteered to speak at a primary school about archaeology, and kept her cynicism in check. Most difficult of all, Leah decided to renounce her stake in the consultancy. She couldn't go back, even though she still loved the guts of the work. There was value in discovery, in learning and recording. But not in the way they'd been doing it, servicing the narrow interests of her old clients.

For eleven days straight, Leah didn't suffer an attack, and she allowed herself to hope. Little by little, the maintenance of Affable Leah felt less like a chore. But on the twelfth day she woke up on a long-haul passenger bus, rolling down some highway. It was just after two in the morning. She didn't have her car keys and there was no cash in her purse.

The bus, it transpired, was an inter-city service carrying her back to a depot near where she lived. She decided not to file a police report about her missing car. How could she? She couldn't state with any certainty that it had been stolen. More likely, she'd chanced on some no-hoper and had just given it over.

Every day was another prospect for taking back control, but the absences kept occurring. In the map of her memory, there were locations now that were simply null, as if some crooked process had deemed them unimportant and countenanced their demolition. But those missing spans *were* important. She lost her paternal grandmother's pearl earrings, the only heirloom that had passed down to her from that side of the family. Despite everything, Ruth had always conceded that Leah's father's mother was a kind woman, and the earrings were the 'something old' that Leah had chosen to wear on the day she'd married Donny. After they vanished, Leah spent mornings visiting pawn shops and jewellers, but it was no good.

Leah had spent a career working with objects. She knew that some special things were the bones over which memories and meanings were layered. Stories had sequences, parts deployed in order. Lose some of the parts, or scramble the sequence, and what remained was a useless mess.

Almost a full week would pass without an attack, but then some days it would happen twice. Every time she came back from an absence it was sickening, as she realised that moments before, she had not been in charge of herself.

◆

In desperation, she took her mother's advice.

Leah found the old priest singing quietly to himself as he distributed hymn books along the ends of each pew. He was dressed casually in a bottle-green jumper and open-collared shirt, but she remembered the careful way he moved, and the reedy timbre of his voice as he'd delivered one of his marathon homilies, back in the day.

The red-brick building remained squat and austere, the interior lit dimly through crude stained-glass windows that inspired no-one. A whiff of incense and some grubby finger-marks around the holy water stoup took Leah back to the last time she'd been here, under protest, just before she'd left for good. To her teenage self, church had been purely tedious. But returning now, Leah was struck by how much this place must have meant to her mother. It had become Ruth's community, and at the same time her sanctuary from others. Even though he'd arrived at the parish a decade before Ruth and Leah, Father Marras had remained an outsider, too: a bookish theologian, posted to a backwater town whose inhabitants were largely descended from Irish migrants fleeing the Great Hunger. The people here could be spiteful, and now that Leah was grown, she could recall some of the remarks she'd overheard but not understood back then. Snide whispers: *The food's edible, but would it kill Ruthy to get some magazines, hang some posters? At least turn the godforsaken radio on. Poor thing – I try not to cringe when she asks if I want my fish battered.*

'Hello, Father,' Leah said.

She watched him as recognition dawned. 'Leah.' His posture relaxed, shoulders settling into a deep hunch. He'd been old when she left, and now he was ancient. 'It's a joy to see you.'

They sat down next to each other, and Leah told the priest her story. Details of every attack. Her search, fruitless, for a sensible explanation. It came tumbling from her: . . . *And then*

I must've told the doctor what happened, with Mum. How she had to run, to make sure I was safe . . .

She spoke of her fear, and held nothing back: . . . *I can't do my job – and I keep giving stuff away. Soon it'll all be gone. Without money, what good am I to anyone? To Donny . . .*

It was a forensic account. It took her the better part of half an hour.

When she was done, Father Marras bowed his head, and she wondered if he was thinking or praying. When he looked back up at her, he only said, 'Interesting.'

'Mum says it's God working through me.'

The old man considered this. 'I'd be setting a poor example if I dismissed the possibility.'

'Then I need your help. Please.' She ground her teeth together, hating what she'd come here to ask. 'I need an exorcism.'

Father Marras made a grunting noise. He might have been stifling a cough. 'I don't think that's going to work.'

'I've tried everything else. I'm telling you, I'm at my wit's end.'

He shook his head. 'What I mean is, if you awoke in pools of blood . . . If you were muttering curses, then an exorcism might be worth the attempt. But Leah, when you suffer one of these occurrences, you do good. If this really is possession, then it's as your mother says. And it isn't given to me – to anyone – to cast Him out.'

Leah folded at the waist, head in hands. Deep, angry shame, a long-forgotten feeling, roiled inside. Her attacks had driven her here, back to everything she'd repudiated. Consumed with self-pity, she had begged this man to banish his own god; a god she didn't believe in.

She wept. Even as she gave herself over to sorrow, part of Leah marvelled at the feeling. She couldn't remember ever crying, but she supposed she must have when she was young. The priest sat by her side, squeezing her shoulder, compounding her humiliation.

It took a long time for composure to return, or at least it seemed that way. She was taking heaving breaths, and she tried to concentrate on drawing air in slowly, exhaling slowly. She wiped her eyes with the back of her hand.

To allow her time, perhaps, the priest said, 'When we speak about the afterlife, we tend to imagine it as a wonderful place. But older religions had more complicated cosmologies. We borrow from the Jews, and the Jews borrowed from the Sumerians, who believed that there are seven discrete heavens, and seven earths, too. And that what goes on up there creates little ripples for those of us stuck here.'

'*The Divine Comedy*,' Leah said, remembering a long-ago Classics course she'd taken. 'What's-his-face. Dante.'

'Like Dante, yes,' said the priest, unable to mask his surprise. 'What's your point?'

'I suppose that . . . existence is complicated. It is not for us to know all that there is, much less understand it. Perhaps we are in one of the heavens right now.'

'Is that what you think?'

'No,' he said, frowning. 'I don't think this is any kind of paradise.'

Gingerly, the priest knelt. He placed his hands on hers and spoke softly. 'Heaven or earth, I can't tell. But ask yourself: during these episodes, have you been hurt? Really hurt?'

Leah weighed the question, casting for the truth. 'No,' she said.

'Have you hurt anyone?'

She shook her head, more certain. 'No.'

Behind the rheum in the priest's eyes, there was something like gladness. 'Then celebrate,' he said.

She waited, but there was nothing more for her here. As she studied the varnished whorls of the bench in front, she felt him withdraw, heard the sound of steps receding. The swing of a door shutting.

For a while longer she sat, conscious of something new. Frightening, in its way, but not malicious. If she allowed it time, if she could refrain from snuffing it out, one day it might reveal itself.

When she was ready, Leah grabbed the side of the pew and levered herself up. On her way outside, as she passed through the vestibule, she slowed. For three heartbeats she considered the donation box.

In the diagonal glare of the early summer evening, Leah walked the streets of her old home town, arriving at her mother's front door.

Leibniz and Newton Take the Train

Haruka's nose pressed against the suit jacket of the passenger in front. She thought about Gottfried Leibniz. It was the same each morning. Wait in the crush to board the train, northbound on the Chiyoda. During peak, the line ran at 181% of capacity. At Yushima, where Haruka boarded, commuters assembled in front of the marks indicating just where the train would stop. A stable formation, until the doors opened and the attendants began scrummaging from the back of the platform to wedge in more passengers. Haruka was proud of the efficiency.

The soap-concealed cigarette reek of the salarymen, the jostle of the train and the press of humid bodies all around her, the warmth and the tightness in her chest when she inhaled dank air: some part of her was conscious of it all. But she did not give those impressions licence. They could not access the muscles that controlled her face or her hand that loosely gripped the pole. Even though it might feel otherwise, there was a vast distance between herself and the man at her back.

Haruka had been in high school when she first learned about Leibniz. The old physicist had held that without matter, there could be no void. Emptiness was only bestowed with meaning by the position of the bodies amongst it, just as love could not exist without lovers. No kinship without family. No society without citizens.

Then there was Isaac Newton, Leibniz's contemporary and great rival. Newton had disagreed most emphatically. He wrote that absence had its own existence, independent of any countervailing presence. But Haruka always thought that Leibniz's view was the more Japanese. Each bond had an anchor, each train a station, each obligation a debtor. Emptiness could only be appreciated because the universe was full. Newton was *hikikomori* in his physics: a shut-in loner.

◆

The village of Haruka's childhood had seemed full, to her. Nine days after she graduated high school there had been an occurrence at Fukushima, not so far away. Afterwards, the discussion continued for weeks until finally, the government announced that it was not safe to remain. There was an emptying, and Leibniz might have said that the place ceased to exist. Her parents moved north, to a seaside village in Aomori Prefecture. Haruka travelled south, to Tokyo and university. At the start of each year, her colleagues returned to their birthplaces to spend a day or two, but Haruka could not. And now she worked to prevent further dislocations of the type that had claimed her home.

◆

In minutes she would arrive at Kita-Senju, for the switch to the calm and comfort of the Tsukuba Express. At Kashiwanoha, a quick bus ride and an even shorter walk would have her at the Institute. Point to point to point. She was fortunate to have her research fellowship. Fortunate, also, that her morning journey was not too long by Tokyo standards.

The day began to unspool as soon as she arrived, following the usual patterns. She greeted the space, turning on lights and checking the status of the corrosion test loop that had been left to run overnight. Half an hour later, Sato-sensei bustled in with his briefcase. Haruka followed him into his office and delivered an update. After that, she took her seat at the workstation near the stairwell, and continued verifying datasets that had been supplied by an American facility. The Americans, too, were developing a molecular trap for minor actinide extraction. It would be to everyone's benefit if their findings could be shown to match those of the Institute.

Through the glass window of his office, Haruka could see Sato-sensei typing. She didn't know much about her supervisor, and she assumed there was not all that much to know. He was in his fifties, with a mop of greying hair that was too long and unruly to allow anyone to mistake him for a regular salaryman. He had a wife and a child, a little boy. He had a car – a Honda. On his desk, there was a photograph of Sato-sensei clasping hands with Asimo, the famous robot. Sato's hobby was baseball, but he didn't play.

◆

At lunchtime she walked to a nearby Family Mart and purchased onigiri. Besides Sato-sensei, the clerk at the store was the only person she would speak to that day. It was a fine autumn afternoon, not too humid, and she took her lunch to the municipal park and found a bench next to the rose garden. A Tuesday, so the local police orchestra was practising in the amphitheatre nearby. Recently they had taken to ending their sessions with a rendition of 'What a Wonderful World'.

Haruka felt a momentary pang about buying her food. She could have risen earlier and cooked her own lunch – a bento that would have been prepared with greater consideration. But academics didn't care too much about those things, and most of her colleagues without wives did the same as Haruka and purchased their lunch from a *kombini*, or from one of the vendors lining the arcades that fed off the subway tunnels. She studied the triangular shape of the rice ball, wrapped tightly in nori, and thought about methods of containment. Haruka took small bites, noticing the chewiness of the seaweed.

Tokyo had slow, cool bubbles dotted through the concrete, like the park in which she sat, and for the most part Haruka enjoyed living here. Had she followed her parents north, she would have needed to find a job as an office lady. Now that she was in her late twenties, people would have started referring to her as a Christmas cake, meaning that she was sitting on the shelf, growing stale. Her parents would feel obliged to send her on arranged group dates with other young people. But here, no-one bothered her, and there were plenty of women who delayed.

Sometimes on the weekends, when she had a spare afternoon, she would read visual novels on her computer. The ones made for women, typically concerning a high school student trying to win the affections of one of the popular boys. At critical moments during the story, the reader was presented with options for how the protagonist should respond. She didn't exactly read these tales for the romance. And the sex was not as graphic as in the versions written for *otaku* – although there were exceptions, and she would respond to those scenes in different ways, depending on her disposition at the time. What she most enjoyed was the finite number of choices the reader was offered to direct the story. In a given instalment, there might be seventeen possible endings, and once all permutations had been explored, it was possible to perfectly control the main character's destiny. This felt like as much choice as a person could want.

As for Haruka, she knew what was expected of a wife, and she could guess at the costs and benefits. The way she lived now, there was no time for such things. Science gave her what she needed.

◆

After lunch, she took an hour to read. Haruka found this painstaking, since most of the literature in her field was yet to be translated into Japanese. The mouth in her mind was the wrong shape, and it stumbled over names like Bruce Moyer, Alexander Ivanov, Vyacheslav Bryantsev, not to mention Einstein, and of course, Leibniz. She spent her days thinking about the efficient disposal and containment of americium, europium. There was no such thing as nipponium. Or if there was, it was yet to be discovered and named.

The late afternoon and evening were for writing up the results of Sato-sensei's investigations. Her supervisor was hopeful that this year he would have something to announce, a contribution that would reflect well on the Institute. For that to happen, their work – his and Haruka's – needed to be entirely free from error. The reputation of Japanese nuclear science had been severely damaged by the disaster, and even more so by the subsequent findings regarding TEPCO's lapses in judgement. Whatever they delivered would not only have to advance the field, it must be incontrovertible.

◆

When she had been at the lab for about fourteen hours, Sato-sensei pushed back his chair and collected his things. As he emerged from his office, Haruka swallowed. In her loudest, clearest voice, only slightly hindered by disuse, she called to him. *O-tsukaresama deshita* – you must be tired.

Once he had left, she set about powering down the machines and locking up. She enjoyed this time, and the small rituals of departure. She double-checked the settings on the loop to ensure she hadn't overlooked anything, but even so there was a moment of uncertainty, like cresting a hill, as she pulled the lab door shut behind her. Even when taking care, people were unreliable, and it was in moments such as these that she felt her humanity.

◆

That night she was lucky, and she walked onto the platform a few minutes before the 11:37 pm semi-express. When the train arrived, she found a carriage that was almost empty, with a pair of crumple-shirted office workers nodding off down the far end. But Haruka was not alone. Leibniz was with her once more, commenting on the ambient temperature and, notwithstanding the apparent stillness of the air, describing all of the particles jiggling and crashing around their heads. A few seats further down, Newton sat sullenly, inspecting his puffy fingers and chewing his lip.

When Leibniz spoke Japanese, it was with a thick Teutonic accent. He occasionally spoke to her in German, too, or some pidgin language that sounded to Haruka like German, imploring her to understand something, perhaps something about her work. But at those moments she couldn't comprehend him. Naturally she couldn't – she was aware that this version of Leibniz was a product of her own mind, and she could not gift herself understanding so easily.

Yushima station rushed at the train, enveloping her carriage on all sides, and Haruka braced against the deceleration. The usual announcement was made, and the doors parted with a hiss. Silently, she mouthed a goodbye as she stepped off, exiting like the last drop of liquid from an empty cup.

She encountered no-one on her walk home. When she had climbed the four flights of stairs to her apartment and let herself in, she stopped to listen. It was as quiet as this city ever became. She freed her hair from her ponytail and placed her bag on its shelf in the entryway.

Every day, at the beginning and the end, this was what remained: Haruka's tiny mansion. In the main room she could spread her arms wide without touching a wall. It was immense, beyond all understanding or ease.

Third Heaven

Third Heaven is too crowded for Genevieve's taste. For the solitude, she frequents the lost hour: that missing beat at the start of summer when modern clocks leap forward, and old ones nag for a winding.

It started over breakfast, some weeks earlier. Genevieve – Vee to her late husband – had been trying to force down a slice of dry toast, but the light was wrong, and one of the carers had taken her aside to explain that management had disappeared a whole hour.

The time surrendered fell between two and three am. Had they a choice, most of the living would have given the minutes over to sleep. But Genevieve, a librarian pre- and post-mortem, catalogues what else has been foregone: arguments (Dewey: 168.1), late-night snacks (641.3), unaired infomercials (659.1). Children scheduled for conception during that hour will never exist. Drunken declarations of love will remain un-uttered. Genevieve tuts as she works, flipping through index cards for a destroyed collection.

No-one else in this place seems to care. The badminton players, for instance, don't worry about what has been left behind. Even though they are just as dead as she is, they have maintained their fluency with *now*, always pestering Vee about the weekly schedule. Suggesting classes. In the afterlife, countless diversions have been made available (pottery; line dancing; Microsoft Excel for beginners), but Vee hasn't bothered to explore.

The staff reassure her that an hour will be added to the end of summer, to balance the ledger. But that is a different span, full of unrelated happenings. For those who had a need, it's no recompense. They are ignorant, but Vee knows. In felt-tip pen, she scribbles notes on the walls of a moment:

This is a hotel cook, fatigued, working the breakfast shift. Seven seconds from now, he will scorch his hand against the grill.

Vee stops to regard what she has done. The pen falls from her hand, becomes a chair. She sits, even though there's no need to catch her breath. The concept of rest has no unified meaning in this place, but there's an ache in her back that demands attention.

◆

'She doesn't remember much,' someone is saying. No, not just someone – Vee recognises the lazy diphthongs, dropped Ts and nasal resonance of the nurse who puts Vee to bed most nights, and occasionally helps her into the shower. It must be evening. Vee glances over to the doorway and the corridor beyond. A step behind the nurse, a young woman whose face Vee doesn't recall taps something into one of those flat computers that have replaced clipboards.

'Genevieve can be lucid at times.' The nurse, again. Although she must be in her forties, make-up can't conceal the acne on her cheeks, which is one reason Vee thinks of her as Nurse Pimple. Her fringe hangs lopsided, obscuring one of her eyes, which is impractical and to Vee's way of thinking, makes her look like a drug user. Vee glowers, and the computer-tapper at least has the grace to look embarrassed. The door swings closed, clicking as the latch finds its recess, and everything is dark again.

What awful talk. Vee isn't deaf, or stupid, and nothing has been lost. She is trying to stop a tablecloth from blowing away, or— No. What's most important is her ability to learn. She understands more with each passing day.

Since arriving, Vee has heard things that are not to be told, that no woman or man is permitted to repeat. But as below, so above: those in charge never cogently explain themselves, and seldom speak of anything important.

Every day is more or less the same in here, but that's alright, because surely there can't be many days left. This heaven is a converted manor house, set halfway up a small mountain, and things are kept ship-shape for the most part. In the daytime, a porthole window illuminates the subtle gradations of beige and white in Vee's room. Everything is smooth to the touch. All corners have been rounded off. Back down the hill, there used to be more colour, but in this place, the nearest one comes to red is the pastel pink of the refectory wall. There is no blood here: none of the residents have any to spare. If one were to cut open poor Mr Harris in room twelve – a butter knife would do the job – he would probably leak saline.

The question of daylight saving is only one element of a larger problem. Vee tears clippings from the newspaper, and jots down notes about callers on talkback radio. Back on the plains, lives are still being lived. The purpose of Genevieve's voyeurism, if that's what it amounts to, is to compile a larger data set on which to base conclusions. She ought to know why she's here. The staff won't answer properly, so it falls to her.

◆

Once the morning fog has burned off, the view from the upstairs drawing room is spectacular. The ground drops away abruptly, re-establishing itself far below as a semi-ordered flatland of houses and trees and streets, stretching to the ocean. But spending so much time pointed downhill is discouraged. To remind Vee of this, Cassiel visits her now and then, and chides her. 'Gen-eee-vieve!' With his French West-African inflection, the syllables string out like the start of a nursery rhyme, forming a disjunct melody. 'Come away from there. It is time to work.' He is slender, a head taller than Vee, and laughter lives in his eyes.

He beckons her away from the large window, and time passes, and the now-familiar smell of disinfectant tells her that she has been returned to her room. Vee looks up, to check that he is still with her. She finds herself in semi-repose, in her electric bed complete with buttons and pneumatics, with articulated segments that can be raised and lowered, but which remains in want of a comfortable pillow.

Cassiel is manipulating her left leg, pressing his fingers against the flat of her foot, and asking her to resist. The situation is somewhat undignified, but that doesn't bother Vee. Cassiel has a familiar way about him, and he is the only carer whose real name Vee can recall. In other circumstances his visit might be welcome, but this time he's interrupting. Her work must come first, and she grunts to let him know she's had enough.

Palms outward, he waves his hands back and forth in front of his chest, which she takes to be an apology. The next time she checks, Cassiel is gone.

When she first found herself here, Vee kept expecting to meet the manager, or at least a high-level functionary who could give her a proper welcome. But management lurks somewhere out of frame, promulgating changes to the routine without prior notice, as with the introduction of daylight saving time.

For the most part, Vee's fellow residents confound her. There are many Christians here, of various persuasions. But, she suspects, also Buddhists, Muslims, Hindus, Rastafarians, Jews, Sikhs, Taoists, Wiccans, a few Satanists, and even atheists. Some inhabitants have formed a prayer group. They meet fortnightly in the non-denominational chapel, which is really just a normal room with a skylight and a lectern. Vee is not interested. Post-death, religious questions are basically moot, and she has other ways to search for meaning.

When one of the other residents shares an anecdote about some young relation, Vee can lose whole afternoons imagining herself into their lives, until she inhabits them from within. The other day, she heard a story about a guide, trapped on a tourist island by her own inertia. Later, from her bed, Genevieve had railed, urging that young woman to make a scene, storm out, fling red wine in the faces of the guests.

In life, Vee did all the things that others expected, practising deference. Now, it pleases her to watch other strategies play out. She flicks through lives and here and there stops, inspects.

◆

On the lawns below the main residence, the badminton crew are playing six-a-side, lurching this way and that to keep the shuttlecock airborne. They are a picture of spry health, but time has dulled their competitive instinct. For them, the rally is everything.

Genevieve has allowed herself to be outside, and observes the players in the conventional way, through unborrowed eyes. Cassiel has asked her to work on being present: feeling the air around her, which at this moment means registering the drop in temperature as a bank of clouds passes overhead. She is told that this concentration, this noticing, will help with her disorientation.

Upon her arrival, she had done as any good librarian would, and had reached for reference works. This heaven has a respectable collection. But in their writings about the other side of the veil, the supposed experts had all laboured under the same difficulty: still corporeal, they were just as ignorant as Vee. Occasionally, one of them appeared to have been granted an incomplete, grainy vision of the truth. But there was nothing about badminton, and a lot of silliness besides. Winged beings, clouds thick enough to tread on, lush oases, and virgins. Genevieve can't see any use for a virgin.

The cool change has something to tell her, after all. Fat raindrops start to fall, and a couple of players hurry to pull the net poles from the ground, but they needn't bother. The ground staff will come to their rescue, sooner or later.

◆

When the opportunity next arises, she asks Cassiel about his life below.

'I think this is a very *rude* question.' He feigns offence, shaking his index finger at her, but Vee waits him out. They sit together in the lounge, which is large and tastefully appointed except for the linoleum floor, and on a side table between them are two cups of sage-scented tea. Each time Vee twists and reaches to claim her cup, relief courses down the right side of her back.

As they sip, she re-registers Cassiel's blackness, his African-ness. He is novel, to Vee. Well into adulthood, Vee had practised the genteel xenophobia of the ethnically homogenous, well-to-do eastern suburbs of the city below. If you saw a foreigner at the produce markets, you nodded politely. But in private, a detailed hierarchy was so well understood that it was rarely given voice. In death, Vee is less ignorant, less bigoted, but there is no way to atone. She can only change the future, or perhaps not even that.

'I look after my little boy,' Cassiel says. 'I look after my wife. And I try to have some fun.'

Vee is not sure what she is meant to take from this. 'How does that help?' The question comes out more harshly than she'd meant it to.

Cassiel seems perplexed. He hesitates, before replying, 'We do what we do, and we learn what we learn.'

'But . . . if you could visit yourself when you were alive, what would you say?'

He puts down his cup, and perhaps she has upset him.

Before he can respond, she hurries on. 'I know that I can be exhausting, with all my questions. But you listen. You are kind to me, in your own arrogant way.'

'Arrogant . . . You call me arrogant?' For a moment he seems furious, but he can't sustain it. Eyes closed, he squeezes the arm of his chair, and his shoulders jolt up and down, silently at first, but soon the sound of his amusement makes others turn to look.

Vee raises her hand to her mouth. When they part, they are both smiling.

After he leaves, muttering excuses about other business that cannot be ignored, she drifts, and when she is herself again, she finds that she has been returned to her bed, dressed in a nightgown, and positioned on her side to face the curtained window. The change is too abrupt. Vee draws her knees towards her chest and squeezes her eyes shut.

She is driven backward, into her old life. She doesn't mean to do that, but sometimes a memory insists.

Vee is in the yard, trying to stop the tablecloth from blowing away—

Clark. It's embarrassing how long she's gone without thinking of him. He hasn't arrived at this heaven, and Vee can only assume he's made it to one of the others. Travel is not allowed without a compelling reason, and she hasn't tried to obtain a permit. Truth be known, most of the time Vee is happy in her own company. She loves Clark, but she gave him a long life, as did he for her. She hopes that wherever he's ended up, he is content, and learning to look after himself.

◆

'Why are they serving pudding? I haven't finished my meat.'

[Sound of plates being cleared. Cutlery is thrown into a plastic tub.]

'What's that?'

'You're much too slow, they can't wait forever.'

'Can I get you anything else, Genevieve?'

'What kind of heaven is this? What kind of heaven?'

'What's wrong with her?'

'She thinks she's dead again.'

'Are there any more nectarines?'

'I'm sorry, Victor, we've run out.'

'Lydia's got one. She had one last night, too.'

'You're not dead, love. You're just old.'

'They *told* me. They said I was in heaven . . .'

'They call this place Third Heaven, for some stupid reason. There's a whole chain of them.'

'Should've called it God's Waiting Room.'

'Where's Clark?'

'Where's the fruit bowl gone?'

'Oh, now, he *is* dead, love.'

'Can I take your plate?'

◆

Vee is in the yard trying to stop the tablecloth from blowing away. It is a hot day in spring, and Clark has been out with the mower. Grass cuttings swirl and stick to Vee's bare calves. They are putting on a barbecue for the neighbours.

—But. This wallowing in her own history is unproductive. She already knows what she knows. She – and here she realises that she's inadvertently reached for Cassiel's words – has learned what she has learned. It's the lives of others that will lead her to new ends. What she needs is fresh content, so when she is done with sorrow, and with more than a few misgivings, she makes her way back to the library.

The search is not straightforward. For every life Vee really sinks into, there are others that spit her out almost immediately. Vee would like to believe that every human is afforded dignity, but deep in the catalogue stacks, she has found that it isn't so. It's an awful conclusion, once the full weight of it presses down, and Vee searches in vain for some loophole—

—except, no: Genevieve is sitting alone in a wheelchair, under the tree. In Third Heaven, if one has been placed outside, one is usually under the tree, but most of the time she puts it out of her mind, taking the shade for granted.

The music has started up again, and her backache has returned. She thinks of herself as an old woman, and so she is. Others imagine themselves to be younger. Vee wishes she could simplify the almanac of her body just a little.

It doesn't matter any more, her neighbours say when they see her working. *Nothing does!* When she hears this, Vee feels like an enthusiast playing with model trains. But she is hardly the only person with idiosyncrasies. At least she can speak, unlike the large contingent here who've given up the habit. In the evenings some of them hold concerts, forming an orchestra whose membership is always changing, and they bring forth music composed during the day, the notes skimming over rocks until they collect at the top of the mount. Infrequently, vocalists layer wordless, plaintive melodies over the top of the instruments, and on these occasions, Genevieve pauses her work and listens until the quiet returns.

After the concerts, the players drift off in smaller groups, or are wheeled back to their rooms. They have lost the need for conversation. What is left to communicate that can't be said better through music? Genevieve supposes it makes at least as much sense as what she is doing.

And there are others, like Cassiel, who can leave and return, and who continue to busy themselves with service. Word comes from somewhere on high that there will soon be an influx of new arrivals. A few self-important types form a welcoming committee. In the absence of clear direction, some people will want to help, and some people will want to take charge.

If Vee has learned anything from all the lives she has catalogued, it's that exertion is terrible, but its absence is worse. No search means sitting in the shade of a tree, forever, mourning something incapable of being named.

Cassiel returns to her, and this time his impatience is genuine. Vee can tell that he is fatigued. Behind her back, Vee makes a flicking motion with her hand, dispelling a theory she's been tinkering with.

'I can be caring,' she says. 'I grew up with a bird in the house, and every night I would drape a blanket over its cage, and I never forgot. On the other hand, when I was nine, I contracted varicella – the chicken pox. My little sister was sweet to me, then, fetching damp towels and making up silly rhymes to distract from the itching. But then I started to recover, and she became sick – and I spent the next week avoiding her, because I was afraid she'd re-infect me.'

'What are you trying to find?' he asks her.

Vee grimaces. 'I'm often confused. Oh.' She shakes her head. 'Sometimes I get all muddled up.'

'I think that is not very unusual. And no reason to fear.'

'I suppose you're right.' Vee takes a breath, and as she does so, time jolts forward, like the start of a fairground ride, and she knows she will be leaving soon. 'But my project – I'm close.' Late or not, it must still be possible to understand where she is, where she's been.

Vee brushes her thumb across the fingers of her left hand. 'I'll take one more journey,' she says, and peers into her palm as if she were reading an index card. 'Then I'll be done.'

She is approaching something vital. Muttering, oblivious, Vee applies herself to her task, collecting moments like shards of tile, laying them out in patterns that please her, that make meaning.

◆

Her room, again. Vee doesn't know what time it is, but the lights are off. Under the blankets there is a wet feeling. She sobs, and then there is a keening, long and loud, punctuated by stuttering inhalations. The sounds coming from her throat scare her.

She is alone, beyond reach and hearing. And then the door opens, and a woman's silhouette draws close. A light flickers on, and through her anguish, Vee recognises Nurse Pimple by her lopsided fringe.

The nurse shushes, and the nurse coos, as if tending to an infant. It is patronising in the extreme, and it allows Vee to cultivate a feeling of indignation as she reaches for a tissue and wipes her nose with a trembling hand. As soon as her breathing is under control, she says, 'I want to see my daughter.'

Perhaps it is the lateness of the hour, but the nurse seems cross. She purses her lips. 'You don't . . . you've never . . .' She fiddles with something at the side of Vee's bed, and turns away to pour water into a plastic cup.

'My daughter . . .' Vee knows that she should insist. It's not right to keep people locked away from family, but then again, she senses that no-one in this place is without fault. Vee is riddled with weakness. There must be a reason.

'In the morning we'll call your sister again, if you like. But it's very late, Genevieve. Try and sleep, okay?'

None of this is right. If Clark were here, he'd sort it out, but Vee can't find the words. The hopelessness makes her sob again, and although it mortifies her, Vee reaches forward.

She is being held. Nurse Pimple is holding her, and Vee is allowed to cry. Allows herself to cry. It's permissible, given the circumstances.

◆

Her mind holds memories cut sharp like stones, ready to snag, and – oh, the trip they take, for their honeymoon. They travel by rail from Adelaide to Broken Hill, and then up into the Blue Mountains, to a charming little town. Laura? No, Leura! Clark leads her down into a valley, and shows her the Leura-birds.

He is handsome and eager, and they have days and days alone in a cottage, and on the trains, to learn.

They settle into their marriage. Tangled up with the happiness, over the course of years, there is a recurring sequence of joy, and preparation, and bloody disappointment. Genevieve only weeps the first time. On that day, Clark rushes from work to meet her at the hospital, to hold her, to tell her that they are still young, and it will be different. There will be a next time: how can there not be? Once she feels well enough to walk, a nurse – another blasted nurse – ushers her through reception and outside to the waiting car. They want her gone, she can tell. As if her failure might contaminate the other women.

In time, she finds consolation. Once everything settles, she persuades Clark to let her go back to work. It will be better than moping around the house all day, and she can still get dinner on the table. She finds a job at a library, which brings a useful feeling with it. And then Vee's younger sister has offspring, and then *they* have offspring, and Vee loves them dearly.

Much later, at Clark's funeral, they can only fill a quarter of the church. His friends from the bowling club (those who are left) and some neighbours, and her sister's family. He is remembered fondly by those in attendance. The service begins at mid-morning, and the wake wraps up around two, and to Vee, as an expression of loss, it feels wholly insufficient.

But before that – logically it cannot be afterwards – Vee is in the yard trying to stop the tablecloth from blowing away. It is a hot day in spring, and Clark has been out with the mower. Grass cuttings swirl and stick to Vee's bare calves. They are putting on a barbecue for the neighbours.

A barbecue – the family two doors down are Catholic, and that afternoon, once the mowing is done and the table has been laid, she listens to the sound of children playing. Clark and Vee must be in their fifties. A trade unionist has just become prime minister.

She hasn't been a good host. Dessert is finished, and there are plates to clear, but Clark takes her hand. They watch one another, and she knows:

Shelter

She arrived with a single car-load of stuff. We never found out where she'd been living before. *With some mates*, was all she'd say.

Only one car-load, but it seemed like more once it was inside. For days we – we boys – knocked against new objects as we moved around the house, missing the empty spaces. The bathroom was the worst. We had a hair dryer now. It perched above the medicine cabinet, power cable sweeping down across the mirror to the socket. A drawer below the sink was given over to sanitary products.

She'd found the ad we posted online, and things must have been pretty desperate, because she was still keen even after we'd given her the grand tour. Ours was the worst house in the neighbourhood. Barely any work had been done to the place since the 1950s: the living-room carpet, a faded floral green, attested to that. Tree roots strangled the pipes and the kitchen sink was prone to blocking. The whole house exuded a rotting smell, faint but undeniable, that was impossible to attribute to any one source.

The location suited her, a short walk from her waitressing job. And her rent would be dirt cheap, but that was because she'd be sleeping in a sunroom with no fan, no air-conditioning and louvred windows that were too old and rusted to close the whole way over. A couple of months earlier, a chunk of ceiling had broken off in the hallway outside her room, and the hole still hadn't been repaired. But she knew what she was getting into.

She said she was twenty-seven. Paddy, the eldest of us, was nineteen-and-a-half. We – Paddy, Max and I – were from the easy inner suburbs. The closest we'd come to adulthood was this half year of share-house living, post-high-school.

I watched her. I tried to understand, as she brushed her dark hair out of her eyes. As she cooked a meal. As she stumbled to the bathroom in the morning in a T-shirt and underwear. As she lay on our red beanbag, smoking a bong while we talked, ignoring the news playing on the television. She didn't seem to mind hanging with us. She was a happy person, even when she wasn't stoned. She wanted to be a nurse but her studies were on hold. I wasn't the only one watching: sometimes I caught Max and Paddy staring at her with a nervous intensity. I hoped my face was harder to read.

Would she think we were filthy? There was mould in the shower and dishes would pile up in the sink for weeks at a time, but none of that seemed to faze her. Really, she was as bad as the rest of us. She left hair in the drain. Stray access-ories – scarves, sandals, bags, bracelets – could be found in every room. She couldn't be persuaded to throw out the leftovers she kept in the fridge.

◆

I only saw her get angry once. It was a weeknight. Noah, a high-school friend, had come over to play board games. He'd been trying to grow a beard, and the rest of us were giving him shit about it when she stomped in to the living room.

It was true that we'd made a mess of the kitchen, but usually that didn't bother her if we tidied up afterwards. This time, she shouted, 'Give me a break! I'm not your bloody maid!' She turned upon each of us a look of contempt. She was gone before any of us could think of a way to reply.

'That's our new housemate,' I said. I wondered if she was running late for her evening shift.

'She's nice,' Noah said. 'Hot. You guys are lucky.'

Some nights, after her work closed, she would go out to a club and not return until the next morning. Once every fortnight or so she would bring a man home. Men, not boys like us – men in their late twenties or early thirties, with jobs: carpenter, oil-rig worker, soldier. They would stay for a night, or sometimes for a day or two. We'd pass them in the halls and grunt politely. Mostly I tried to avoid them, but one Saturday morning I was lying on the couch, watching *Rage*, and one of them plonked himself down in our best chair. I wanted to leave the room but I knew how sullen that would have looked, so I stayed where I was.

We watched in silence for a while, and then he made some remark about one of the bands that was playing. His view matched my own private opinion. It showed he had taste, and I couldn't help but murmur agreement. This guy seemed completely at ease in our living room. Not at all embarrassed, as I would have been, if I'd been required to make small talk with housemates the morning after a one-night stand.

'Can't believe she's still asleep,' he said.

'Yeah, she likes a sleep-in.'

He frowned. 'Maybe I'll just head off, then. You'll tell her I said goodbye?'

The idea appalled me. I nodded.

He shifted like he was about to get to his feet. Before I could stop myself, I said, 'Hey. Where did you meet her?'

Settling back into his chair, he dropped the name of a bar in the city that I'd heard of but never been to.

'And how did you . . . What did you say to her? When you met her?'

His smile, which until then had been perfunctory, spread itself into a full smirk. He leaned in conspiratorially. 'I walked over and told her she looked hot. Then I bought her a vodka lemonade.'

'That's it?'

'That's it. A man backs himself. A woman like her, that's what she's looking for.'

◆

Later, I asked Paddy about the men she was bringing home. He said that it didn't bother him. The men were out of our control. We were the ones who got to live with her; they were transient. We weren't competing with the men. Paddy – who was the most knowledgeable about women, because he had an older sister – said that if anything, it showed that she had a healthy sexual appetite.

I had become a bit suspicious of Patrick. He'd started vacuuming the floors on the weekends. Not long after that,

Max announced to us all – he waited until she was in the room – that he'd joined a gym. She flashed him an encouraging smile; Paddy and I rolled our eyes. Max spent more time playing computer games than was good for a person. If he needed to move he could break into a shuffle approximating a jog, but that was his top speed.

As for me, I'd taken to mowing our back lawn, where she had installed a cheap plastic deck chair. The smell of cut grass and two-stroke was exciting: it was the smell of possibility. The noise of the mower and its shudder beneath my hands stripped away every thought, leaving only the resolve to haul this machine up and back across the yard in neat lines. I imagined that to anybody gliding above who bothered to look down, the lighter area of trimmed lawn would stand out, revealing a chart of my progress.

We – we boys – started to fight about stupid stuff, like who was using all of our monthly download quota. Max left passive-aggressive notes on the fridge reminding us that the spaghetti in the clear Tupperware container in the pantry was *his*, and could we please check before using it? Paddy and I responded by making sarcastic references to the Great Pasta Heist. I was almost certain she was the culprit, but I wasn't about to tell that to Max.

In time, we settled into an uneasy truce. Most days it seemed like none of us had a shot with her. That allowed everyone to relax, to treat it as a shared joke. Some evenings when she was at work, we would assemble in the kitchen and, taking turns, we'd relate our newest and best theories about how her affections might be won. 'I'm leaving my bedroom door open,' Max told us one night over a takeaway dinner. 'When I'm reading, when I'm sleeping, when I'm getting changed: all the time.'

'I've noticed that,' Patrick said. 'Hey, how do they make this chicken taste so good?'

'It's a closely-guarded recipe,' I replied. 'The capital-R Recipe, they call it. But I heard it's got something to do with celery salt.'

'One night, she'll be passing,' Max continued softly, as if speaking only to himself. We were used to this; he was a dreamer, only partially residing on the same plane as the rest of us. When his eyes were open, his left eyelid rested just a little lower than the right, which made him look perpetually drowsy. 'She'll be in the mood. Who knows why? She'll see me there. I won't say anything – I'll just nod. And then nature will take its course.' Max's expression was so earnest that Paddy and I couldn't help but laugh. We all took turns practising our best slow, seductive nods.

'You guys have no idea,' I said when the nodding had stopped. 'It's about confidence. You can't wait for the right moment: you've got to make it happen. That's what real men do. That's the sort of thing she'd respect.'

Paddy grinned, delighted. 'Oh! And tell us, master: when exactly do you plan on *making it happen*?'

'I haven't figured that out yet.' Seizing the moment was all well and good, but I needed more time to strategise.

She was not oblivious, and not above using her leverage. 'You fellas have to lift your game,' she would scold playfully if one of us had been thoughtless or unusually unclean. 'This is no way to treat a lady.' Or, when she wanted some small task performed: 'Is there a strong man around here who can give me a hand?'

I became interested in her favourite reality TV shows. I offered to program the video recorder so she wouldn't miss them. One night it was just me and her in her bedroom, drinking cheap gin, no ice, out of glass tumblers. I talked about books and politics and love, even though she wasn't interested in any of those things.

Every day I became less young, and so came nearer to my goal. We weren't sure how long she might stay with us, but she didn't show any sign of wanting to leave. We still didn't really know much about her. She came from a town in south-west Victoria. She peeled her apples before eating them. She snored softly when she fell asleep on the couch. She would preface her arguments by saying, 'But that's just it—'.

What did she think about me? What did she think about?

◆

Towards the end of summer, we had a house party. We invited lots of people from university and school. We hadn't hosted anything this big before, and so we all fretted, in our own ways, about whether anyone would show. She watched us run around getting set up.

When you're young and you're throwing a party, you have the sense that something remarkable is about to happen. Max mixed up a gigantic bowl of punch, heavy on spirits and cheap sparkling wine. A wading pool was inflated and filled with water. I'd been vicious with the lawn, attacked it with the mower until it was patchy stubble.

By eight, we had a backyard full of guests. I spotted her in the kitchen cooking just-add-water pancakes, which felt kind of pointless to me, and a weird entrée to serve at the start of a big night, but when she carried them outside on a large platter, there were plenty of takers.

I kept getting distracted by people wanting to chat. I didn't talk to her the whole night, but I found myself looking around every now and then, to check where she was. For a while she disappeared, and I think she was out the front of the house smoking with some randoms. Half an hour before midnight, I saw her out of the corner of my eye, speaking to Noah, our old school friend. By then he'd been working on his beard for months.

I was just about to go over when she took Noah's arm and started to drag him into the house. He didn't need much convincing.

I glanced over at Paddy and we exchanged a look. He had seen it, too. He shrugged, but I couldn't bring myself to shrug back.

◆

A couple of weeks after that, she told us she was moving home, to Victoria.

She came to my bedroom the night before she left. I'd been reading a detective novel. My head was full of murder and deception, and I wasn't prepared when I opened the door to find her standing there.

'What's happening?' she asked. I shrugged. She might have been stoned. Looking back, she was almost certainly stoned.

'You'll be right,' she said. 'You've got a good thing going here.'

There was something in her voice – not quite sad, or bitter – but it made me realise that I couldn't really know her. My face grew hot. What had led her to us in the first place, and why she was leaving – I hadn't bothered to learn.

'You won't have a problem,' she said, and she gave me a smile. She wandered off down the hall, deeper into the house.

After she left, we – we boys – moved between rooms, missing the things she'd taken.

Next time the lease came up for renewal, we agreed we were done. That good share-house feeling, of being hapless and free, had dissipated. Paddy had started seeing a rich girl who lived in a flat all by herself, so he was hardly ever around. Max was tired of doing his own laundry, and decided to move back in with his mum. And I didn't know why, but I'd had enough. It was time for something new.

The Last Day of Christmas

t was the best of hams, it was the worst of hams. On Christmas Day it had been pulled, glaze-sticky, from the barbecue, and carved into slices so big they covered both of Juliette's palms. The whole family had set happily to work. Now, as the new year approached, the meat that remained was slimy. And everyone was sick of eating.

It was the final day of the Test, and her dad was sunk deep into the sofa when the doorbell rang. Juliette's grandparents on her mother's side, in town for a late visit, weren't expected for another half hour.

'Come *on*,' said Dad, rubbing at the skin above his cheek. The gold tinsel the kids had stuck along the top of the television was drooping, and now it was hard to follow the play when the ball was hit to fine leg. A reporter kept interrupting the match to show footage of trees burning somewhere, then shots of fire trucks and people crying, but soon enough the cricket was back on, and the playing surface ringing the pitch looked healthy and green.

From the kitchen, Juliette's mum must have heard Dad complain. She came to stand in the doorway, her eyes darting from him to the front door and back again. 'It's once a year.'

Every day of December had been lived in service to Christmas, but Christmas was over. The kids lolled around, slack somehow. Near Dad's feet, Juliette was playing with the Lego set she'd got from Santa. Libs, the oldest, had yesterday declared Lego to be kids' stuff, but even so she was helping to rearrange the town Juliette had built. In the far corner of the room, a plastic tree sagged under the weight of too many baubles, angels, decorative school projects from the last week of term, and a rope of Christmas lights that didn't shine any more when you flicked the switch. Toby, the middle child, was in his room gaming. Muffled gunfire sounds turned his closed door into the skin of a drum.

Still, when Grandma and Pop shuffled in, the whole family assembled. There was hugging and the usual commentary about how tall the children had grown. Juliette's mum smiled hard and led everyone out the back.

The pergola took up almost a third of the yard. Cream concrete tiles, set at diagonals, ran from the brown-brick exterior of the house to the lip of the swimming pool. Overhead, translucent plastic, corrugated, warped the sun and took away its sting, but cast distorted half-shadows. For Juliette, the pergola meant sitting on a floppy canvas chair and reaching her arms up towards her plate.

In the middle of the space, their long table was draped with the same red cloth that had served the family through the Christmas season. A wipe-down had restored it to working order, but stubborn discolourations mapped its history. It was hot and still too early for lunch. Juliette gazed at the pool, but the children knew they were expected to remain while the adults talked.

Pop claimed the head of the table, and Gran lowered herself into the chair next to him, facing back towards the house. Juliette ran to a spot down the other end, between her brother and sister.

'How's Juliette going at school?' The question, from Gran, was directed at Juliette's mum.

'Her handwriting's come along. Got her pen licence this year.'

Juliette knew this was a dumb thing to be proud of – her siblings had told her as much – but even so, she beamed when Gran reached over, clasped her hand and said, 'Congratulations.'

'You been watching the cricket?' Poppa asked Toby. The boy looked down and shook his head.

'He's not much of a one for sport,' Juliette's dad replied on behalf of his son. 'Spends most of his time in his room. What are you playing at the moment, the one with all the shooting?'

'*Endless Struggle*,' Toby mumbled. 'And *Reality Quest*. It's retro – just words, no pictures, like video games from the olden days.'

That got Mum's attention. '*Reality Quest*? I thought that was R-18. I watched a story about that on *A Current Affair* last week – you shouldn't be playing that.'

Toby discovered a way to slump further in his chair. 'It's fine, Mum, everyone at school plays it, jeez.'

After that, no-one spoke for a while. Mum stood up. 'Let's have some music.' She squeezed between her chair and the wall, over to the portable speaker on the window ledge, the window open a crack to let the charging cable snake inside. Mum was lean, almost severe, very much like Gran. Libs had the same build, and with them here together, it was like watching a time-lapse of one person. Juliette and Toby took after their father. *Puppy fat* was how everyone referred to it in Juliette's case.

Libs aimed a dark look at her mother. 'If she plays 'Little Drummer Boy' again I'll fucking lose it.' She said it quiet, so that Mum couldn't hear, but Gran's face collapsed like cracked plaster.

'Time for presents!' Poppa announced. He disappeared inside, and returned carrying a large plastic bag. He moved slowly, and as he passed Juliette she heard the rasp of his breath. 'For you,' he said to Libs, holding out a parcel wrapped in butchers' paper. 'From me and your Gran. Happy Christmas.' He planted a kiss on the top of the older girl's head while she sat still as a stone.

When he was done, Libs tore at the paper to reveal a make-up kit. There were lots of different things inside a clear plastic case, and Juliette wanted to pull everything out to see what was what. She couldn't tell whether her sister liked the present. Libs was fifteen now, and getting good at the adult trick of hiding her feelings.

'Just what she needs,' said Mum.

Toby's present was a long triangle-shaped box, about the length of a ruler from end to end. Even before he tore the paper, Juliette knew what it would be. And yes, it was a block of chocolate. 'Toby Toblerone,' Pop rumbled, looking pleased with himself.

'Thanks Pop. Thanks Gran,' said Toby, but it was Juliette's eyes that grew large.

She had eaten a Toblerone once, a smaller bar, perhaps a year before. She didn't remember the exact taste of it. But looking at the honey-coloured box, she vividly recalled the feeling of the triangle yielding as she chewed. The chocolate was rich, and there were – what – crunchy bits inside. Crunchy and then sticky against your teeth.

Lost in thought, she didn't notice Pop until he was behind her, reaching his arms around to place a large package on the table. 'For you, princess,' he said, and kissed her head. Juliette could feel the puff of his breath in her hair. His hand on her arm felt warm and wet.

The size of the present was encouraging. But when she unwrapped it, removing the sticky tape carefully like she'd been taught, she found a doll.

'The woman at the shop said it's very lifelike. You can feed it,' said Gran.

'You can practise being a mummy,' said Pop.

Juliette scrunched paper in her hand. Dolls were for babies, and she was almost ten. Gran and Pop should have known that. Her mum should've told them.

'Thank you,' Juliette said quietly. She looked at her mother, who nodded and winked. For a few seconds that almost made everything better, but she glanced again at the doll, and the injustice filled her right up. Even a make-up kit like Libs got would have been better, and as for Toby's gift—

'Can I have some of your chocolate?' Juliette asked Toby.

'It's mine,' he replied firmly. Toby was a good brother most of the time, but he was a hoarder. This year his Easter chocolate had lasted into October, tormenting Juliette until Mum threatened to chuck it in the bin.

'*Please*,' Juliette begged.

Mum flashed Dad a look, and he said, 'We're about to eat.'
He marched the yellow box inside. Toby nodded as if justice
had been done.

'What's for lunch?' Pop asked.

'I thought we'd put out some cold plates, and everyone can
make their own.'

'Crackling, and gravy? Roast potatoes?'

Mum frowned. 'We did all that on Christmas Day.'

Juliette said, 'I don't want any more ham. It smells funny.'

Mum put down the stack of plates she'd been distributing.
'I'll make you a peanut-butter sandwich.'

◆

After lunch, Toby took his bike from the garage and wheeled
it out the front. Libs disappeared into her room with her new
present. She'd asked Juliette whether she wanted to come and
watch her try the make-up. Juliette had liked being invited, but
she shook her head. She watched the adults for a minute, and
clutched her doll upside down by the foot, dragging it off the
table as she stood up. 'Are you going to play with baby?' Poppa
asked. Juliette nodded, looking at the pattern the tiles made
under her feet, and ran inside.

She shut the flyscreen door and held still, checking for any
sign of her sister. Hearing nothing, she chucked the doll hard
at the sofa. Sweeping into the kitchen, Juliette began with the
fridge, but it was too full of leftovers. She couldn't see past
the stuff at the front, and it would be hard to shift things in
and out. She turned her attention to the walk-in pantry.

She slid the door shut behind her and found the switch for the light. It was cool, and the sounds of her family were not as loud as her own breathing. The shelving curved around her on three sides, forming a U-shape, and there was plenty of space to turn around. Suspended from the ceiling was a too-bright globe that left after-images when Juliette looked up. She scanned the lower shelves, half hidden in shadow, pushing aside bags of rice and flour. Jars of disgusting curry paste. When she couldn't find what she was looking for, she planted her foot on the second shelf off the ground, grabbed at one of the vertical rails holding everything together, and levered herself upward, hoping that the shelf would hold her weight.

When she stretched tall, her eyes could clear the top shelf. There! – next to a half-drunk bottle of clear alcohol. She leaned out and grabbed for the box. Her hands closed around it, but she'd shifted too far and had to jump clear of the shelf she was standing on. Her feet hit the pantry floor with a slap and her head pulled up centimetres from the hard metal edge of a rail. But in her right hand, she held the Toblerone.

Juliette stood perfectly still. She heard her grandfather's foghorn laugh, but no sound of chairs scraping over concrete. No footsteps.

Examining her prize, turning it over in her hands and feeling the weight inside, she saw a new problem. You were meant to tear a serrated cardboard tab to open the packaging. But if she did, there would be a gap. Later, anyone who looked would know what had been done.

When she pulled at the cardboard covering one of the ends, it started to rip. It was glued too firmly. So she left the box on the floor and ran back out to the kitchen, ducking behind the benches. In the second drawer next to the sink, she found scissors.

Returning to her cave, door closed over, Juliette eased a blade through one of the triangular points at the end of the box. Wiggling it in and along, she cut a breach in the cardboard. When she withdrew the scissors, the gap was hardly visible. She had formed a flap. When she tugged it open she could see silver, and when she tipped the box, the block slid easily.

She peeled at the foil, exposing a single wedge of chocolate. In her left hand she held the box, and her right thumb slid between the end piece and its neighbour.

Juliette paused. She was nine. She understood that some resources were in short supply: time on the computer, toys, the attention of a parent. Chocolate. She thought about Toby, and hesitated. She knew the feeling of losing something precious.

She wiggled her thumb, just testing, and the piece came away more easily than she expected. The wedge dropped to the pantry floor. Her hand reached, but Juliette stopped herself. She stood up, packed the foil back into the box. She tried to close the hinge she'd created, but she must have bent the cardboard too far. When she took her fingers away, the flap sprang open again.

The air felt stuffy here, and Juliette started to shake. She wondered if she could stick the flap back down. There would be something like glue – golden syrup? – here in the pantry. But then the sounds from outside changed. The scrape of a knife over crockery.

There was no more time. Juliette replaced the Toblerone where she'd found it on the top shelf, making sure the tampered end faced back towards the wall. Jumping down, she snatched her prize from the floor. There was another noise, much louder: a crash of spilled cutlery and shattering glass.

Everything happened then. She peeled away a streak of foil and stuffed the chocolate into her mouth. The taste – she remembered it now. It filled her mouth. The piece was too large, and she mashed down with her teeth; breathing quick through her nostrils, it was hard to get enough air. Tears welled and ran down the sides of her nose. And she heard the flyscreen door slide open.

She fled into the kitchen, almost colliding with Dad, who'd run inside to snatch the cordless phone from its cradle on the wall. Snuffling, turning her face to hide her full cheeks and her tears, Juliette swerved into the lounge room.

When she looked outside, she saw Gran lying on the tiles, and Mum crouched over her, shouting something. Poppa stood by, holding his hands to the sides of his head. Juliette watched as he bent down to retrieve a broken bowl. The tablecloth hung like a cape. Half-uncovered, the grey wood of the table looked shabby and wrong. Gran's head rolled, moving funny, and Mum was screaming now.

Libs appeared at Juliette's shoulder. She must have heard the noises, too. The older girl made a huffing sound and wrapped her arms around her chest.

Behind them, Dad was reciting their address. He sounded angry. Juliette turned to look at him and when she caught his eye, he stopped talking down the phone. He walked over to Libs and squeezed her shoulder. 'Take Juliette,' he said. 'Go to your room and stay there till I get you.'

Libs nodded and turned to face her sister. But Juliette was quicker, already in motion, skirting the coffee table. Grabbing her doll from the floor, she bolted down the hall to the bathroom. Inside, she switched the lock.

Ignoring her sister's calls and the jiggle of the knob, Juliette washed her hands. She sobbed. Even the lingering aftertaste of the chocolate was better than anything she could remember eating. A dot of foil fell from her thumb and disappeared down the plughole. She spat brown saliva into the sink. Worried that Libs might smell chocolate on her, she brushed her teeth.

After she'd dried her mouth, she stood facing the wall, running her fingers over the rough edge of her blue towel. 'Little Drummer Boy' sounded in her head: *pa rum pum pum pum*. Unable to think of anywhere better, she placed her doll in the empty bathtub.

When she was ready, Juliette opened the door and walked down the hall. She kept her eyes ahead until she was inside Libs' room. Stepping over piles of discarded clothes, she joined her sister on the bed. The make-up kit was open, its contents spilled over the dressing table.

Ignoring the heat of the day, the girls lay back, feet touching. They drew the sheet over themselves as far as it would go, and settled in to wait.

Reality Quest

You are standing in a field.

The sun shines on your back and a gentle breeze plays over wheat, full-grown and ready for harvest. The air smells sweet and you breathe deeply. You are strong, and hardy, and brave. You are an adventurer.

Enter your age, adventurer:

>>> 15

Reality Quest (© 2018 Fancy Dungeon Studios) contains situations that are inappropriate for children. Please stop playing immediately and notify a parent or guardian.

>>> 22

Aged 22, you are in the summer of your youth. What is your name?

>>> charlotte

Well met, charlotte. Every day a treasure waits, and the only thing wanting is a seeker. Since you were a lad, you have dreamed of setting off on an epic quest. This is your time.

>>> im a girl!

Invalid command. For instructions and a list of basic commands, type 'help'.

Forty yards to the west, at the edge of the field, you see a gate leading to a dirt track. A signpost stands next to the gate like a quiet call.
You are clad in a homespun cotton shirt and leather jerkin. From your belt hang an old, blunt dagger and a pouch containing twenty-five silver pieces.

>>> go to gate

You pass through the gate. Because you are a conscientious sort, you close and fasten it behind you. You were raised on a farm and you know what to do with gates.

>>> look at sign

Atop the post, wooden arrows announce three destinations.
The sign pointing north reads: *Mount Arduous*. You have heard legends of a prize, glorious beyond all imagining, buried deep beneath that mountain. But no-one who has ventured that way has ever returned.
The sign pointing south reads: *Par*. You are a stranger to this land, but you have heard tell of this village. It is reputed to be pleasant enough, with a large stone priory and a market.
The sign pointing west reads: *Rogues Forest*. You think there

is an apostrophe missing from *Rogues*, but you are from low circumstances, educated at home by your well-meaning but unsophisticated mother, and you would not wager your life on it.

>>> go south

You turn southward, the morning sun slanting through the trees.

The path you tread is wide and lined with ancient oaks. Timber and stone bridges span babbling creeks, and twice you stop to slake your thirst with fresh, clear water, melted from a glacier somewhere far away without a name. You feel energised, ready for whatever lies ahead.

After midday, you see smoke rising nearby. Approaching, you make out a homestead set amongst the trees to the side of the path.

You have no pressing need to stop at this place, and you could easily pass by. But whoever lives here might have provisions and information.

>>> go to homestead

You approach and pound your fist on the homestead's sturdy wooden door. Receiving no answer, you follow the line of the building around to the rear, towards the stable and a penned area from which comes the happy snuffling of pigs. You make out a small, gangly fellow dressed in the manner of a peasant. He sees you and waves. 'Hail, stranger!'

>>> talk to peasant

Greetings are exchanged, and you mention you're bound for Par. He tells you that on foot, it's a good three days' journey hence.

'There's naught for me to give a traveller,' the man says. He pauses to scratch viciously at his neck, and you wonder if he carries fleas. 'Might be I could sell you what you need. Food for your journey – let's see, that'd be two silver. A horse, saddled and shod, to speed your way: twenty silver. Or, mayhap, a clever pig? For companionship, and to keep watch while you sleep? Ten silver.'

>>> buy food

You hand over two silver pieces and the man disappears into the homestead. He returns with a sack which he hands to you. Inside are:
1 x large heel of bread;
1 x chunk of corned beef, dry and slightly pungent with age;
1 x half-wheel of cheese, covered in wax.
You nod your satisfaction.

>>> buy horse

The man leads you into the stables. When your eyes adjust to the dimness, you see two horses standing in separate bays. The larger animal is midnight black, with a thin streak of white on its forehead. It snorts proudly and stamps its foot. 'My master's,' the man says, following your gaze, 'and not for sale. For your coin, you can have the other.'

The remaining horse shies as you approach, its rump slamming against the back of the stall. It is white with a grey mane. You can sense its restlessness. 'Olaf's a young colt. Needs a firm hand, but he's swift as a gale. If you can master him, he'll serve you well.'

Money spent, you lead your new horse back out to the path, dismissing the peasant with a wave. You stuff the sack of food inside your shirt to keep it secure, and vault on to Olaf's back.

The horse breaks before you can find your balance. Stretching into a canter, he charges down the path. It takes all your strength and will to stay with him, squeezing your legs into his sides and gripping his neck. By sheer luck you find yourself riding south towards Par. 'Whoa!' you shout, but for naught.

After a time, you learn your horse's rhythms and the going becomes easier. Meadows and woodland rush by on either side. You have never felt more alive.

By mid-afternoon, you and Olaf have reached an understanding. Flagging, the horse drops to a trot. You stroke his neck. 'Good boy.' At the next stream, you pull him up and dismount. You lead your horse to water and, obligingly, he drinks.

You continue on your way until the sun starts to slip between the trees. To your right, you see a clearing that would be a good place to make camp for the night. Or you could ride on, ignoring your growling stomach and Olaf's tired feet.

>>> rest

You tie Olaf to a tree, and he sets to work munching on the surrounding grass. With twigs and flint, you start a fire. You eat your fill of cheese, beef and bread. When you are done, you say goodnight to Olaf and lay yourself amongst fallen fir branches, Belly full. The night sounds soothe you to sleep.

Do you want to save your game?

>>> no

The next morning, you wake with a glad heart. When you open your eyes, Olaf is staring at you, stamping his foot. 'Patience, boy,' you say to him, and laugh.

You ride at a swift, steady pace all morning. At noon you stop for food and water. You are making good time and by your reckoning, you might make Par by nightfall. The thought of food, the company of other folk, and a soft bed fills you with anticipation. You squeeze your feet into Olaf's side, urging him into a gallop, and he responds.

You approach a rise in the road and Olaf attacks it, bolting up the path. But as you crest the hill, you see that the path ahead of you is blocked by a fallen tree, its canopy littering the way with leaves and thick branches. You have a split second to decide: haul back on the reins and slow your horse, or spur him on and attempt to charge through?

>>> slow horse

Descending now, you try to pull up short. At the last moment, caught between his own momentum and your command to halt, Olaf tries to vault the obstruction. The horse's front leg lands in a snarl of wood, and you hear a crack, then a piercing screech, even as you are pitched forward and over Olaf's head.

When you open your eyes again, the sun is low. The left side of your face feels wet and when you raise it from the earth, you see blood.

A muffled, painful call distracts you from your own predicament. Olaf lies beside the tree. Both tree and beast are irredeemably broken. Olaf's leg juts wrongly, shards of bone piercing the skin. At your approach he tries to roll over, but when he moves his damaged leg he shrieks, head flailing back to rest against gravel.

You move to crouch in front of Olaf's face, so that he can see you with his large eye. You murmur soothing words and listen to the heavy panting breath of your friend. Olaf will never walk again, but he could live for days more in agony. You know that you have a hard choice to make.

>>> wtf??

Invalid command. For instructions and a list of basic commands, type 'help'.

>>> this is bullshit

Invalid command. For instructions and a list of basic commands, type 'help'.

>>> heal horse

Even the most gifted physician could not heal your horse.
Alone in the woods, with no medicine or bandages, there is but
one thing you can do for this animal.

Olaf tries to move his head towards your waiting hand, but
the effort must cause a shift in his injured leg, and he screams
again.

>>> don't make me kill olaf

Invalid command. For instructions and a list of basic commands, type 'help'.

>>> run

Invalid command. Movement commands must be attached
to a direction or location.

>>> kill horse

Casting around the brush by the side of the path, you locate
a heavy stone. The effort required to lift it makes you dizzy, but
you carry it over to Olaf. Weeping, you take a last look at your
friend and raise the stone above your head.

>>> stop

You stop what you are doing.

>>> run south

Dropping the stone, you flee. In your haste, you forget your sack of provisions. The screech of the injured animal follows you down the path and the sun sinks until you are running into the black. Blood oozes from the wound on your head.

Hours later, fatigue and vertigo overcome you. You collapse on a low ridge, exposed to the night.

Do you want to save your game?

>>> no

The sun is high when you wake. You remember Olaf, miles to the north, and you sob. But only for a little while, because you are strong. And brave. You are an adventurer.

Picking yourself up, you contemplate your options.

>>> go south

You trudge towards Par. Your head throbs, and pain shoots down your neck and along your arm with every step.

Dizzy and weakened, your pace is slow. It is evening by the time you tread the cobbled street that wends through the centre of Par. Before long, you spy a large two-storey wooden structure. Noise and illumination spill out into the night. Collecting yourself, you swing open the door and step boldly inside. Despite your filthy, bloodstained appearance, the patrons keep their eyes to themselves, continuing their own conversations. Eventually, an older fellow scurries over and looks you up and down.

'Welcome,' he says. 'I am Kannagh.' He has a pinched look, and he emphasises the guttural sound at the end of his name. Your mother always advocated tolerance, but you take an instant dislike to this man. 'You look like you could use a pint, a pie and somewhere soft to lay,' Kannagh continues. 'Two silver for dinner and bed.' He attempts something that might be interpreted as a smile, but his eyes narrow as he waits on your answer.

>>> pay

You hand over the money, realising that you are now down to your last coin. The innkeep leads you to an empty table, and you take stock of your surrounds. It is a soothingly generic location; a kind of ur-inn. Everything one would expect – the sturdy bar, the fireplace, the muttering drunkards – is present and accounted for. Long ago the walls must have been painted white, but the wood smoke has coated everything in dark grit. A staircase ascends to another floor above, and from its banister, you could leap out to swing on the crude chandelier suspended from the roof, if you were inclined to do some swashbuckling.

A beautiful young woman approaches your table bearing a tankard. She is ample of bosom and slim of waist. Her long, blonde hair frames a fine-boned face. Despite your ragged appearance, she smiles as she deposits the tankard in front of you and pauses, as if waiting to see what you will do.

>>> drink ale

You take a hearty swig. Approvingly, the wench says, 'Well met, stranger. You look like you have a tale to tell. I am Gwendolyn. My father, Kannagh, runs this place.' The gutturals sound almost sweet coming from her lovely mouth.

Your evening is starting to improve, but as your own father used to say, attend to business, and joy will follow. Funds now all but exhausted, you realise you must come by more coin. You ask Gwendolyn whether work is to be had in this town.

'Aye,' she replies. 'For a strong, handsome lad such as yourself.' Her gaze lingers over your chest. 'Why even here tonight, I can spy – well. That big fellow yonder—' she points to the bar, where a man sits alone, contemplating his drink, '—Dunn, is the town blacksmith. He's a man of few words, but honest and fair. His last 'prentice met a tragic end not two moons ago: fell into the forge. Could be he'd take you on.' Gwendolyn gives your arm a squeeze. 'Oooh,' she moans.

>>> omfg

Invalid command. For instructions and a list of basic commands, type 'help'.

Gwendolyn winks saucily, and leaves for the kitchen. Your eyes track her shapely bottom as she departs.

You approach the bar and take the seat next to Dunn the blacksmith. 'I am charlotte,' you say in a deep, confident voice. 'I am newly arrived in this land, seeking honest work.

Perchance you could use another pair of hands at your forge?'

Dunn scrutinises you. 'Perchance I could. You'll toil hard, lad, and there's hazard in the flames. But in return I'll pay you three silver a day, and at night you can lay your head on the straw in my stable. What say you?'

>>> yes

You clasp Dunn's hand, sealing the bargain. Now that your immediate future is secured, weariness steals up on you. You drain your tankard and bid Dunn goodnight. You glance around, hoping to catch the lovely Gwendolyn's eye, but she is nowhere to be seen. Sighing, you climb the stairs and find your room.

Do you want to save your game?

>>> no

You awake with the dawn and make your way to the smithy. For the time being, you resolve to do honest work for this man, Dunn. When you are better resourced, you will find your true destiny.

Dunn spoke true when he said the work was hard and dangerous. He neglected to mention the sheer heat that assails a man standing next to an open forge. By evening you are drenched in sweat. Your skin feels tender, as though it has started to roast.

Your new master appraises you, seemingly content with what he finds. 'You'll toughen up soon enough.'

That evening you retreat to your new bed in the stables and the smell of straw and horse dung.

A week passes. Sometimes you take ale after your day's work is done, and you converse with the townsmen. They seem like warm and comfortable folk. When you explain that you are an adventurer, that you are resting here briefly to regather yourself before your next quest, they shake their heads and mutter. There is not much appetite for danger or adventure here.

Do you want to save your game?

>>> no

Another week passes. The terrible soreness in your arms and back recedes somewhat. You begin to frequent the inn almost every night. Ofttimes you share a word with the lovely Gwendolyn. She, alone of all the townsfolk, seems impressed by your resolve. 'I never met an adventurer before,' she tells you.

During your days at the smithy, you are kept busy making horseshoes and ploughshares. Dunn is impressed with your tenacity, and in recognition, he shows you how to fashion a sharp edge from a lump of iron. He says that in your own time you can work on a sword to keep, and for the next five evenings you apply yourself to the task, folding and hammering hot metal and honing your new blade. When you are done, you hang it on the stable wall next to the pallet where you sleep. In the evenings, when your eyes alight on it, your longsword beckons like a quiet call.

To celebrate your achievement, you return to the tavern in high spirits. You drink a toast to what you have accomplished.

Seeing you, Gwendolyn approaches. 'You seem pleased,' she coos.

'The day of my departure draws near,' you reply. 'Soon enough I will leave this town to seek my fortune.'

A frown steals over Gwendolyn's lovely face. 'I have never been further than the pool where I bathe sometimes, no more than an hour's walk from Par. You must have seen so many wonderful, dangerous things on your journey.'

In truth, you are new to adventuring. You've had not so much as a single battle. You've never seen a real monster. You could admit as much to Gwendolyn. Or you could lie, spinning tall tales of your bravery in the face of mortal danger.

>>> lie

You recount to the lovely Gwendolyn the fictitious tale of the time you saved a village, single-handed, from a group of fierce bandits. Her eyes grow wide. 'Such valour! Please, charlotte, tell me more. I beg you! Only—'

'Only what?'

'Only, it is very crowded in here, don't you think? Perhaps if we retired to my room . . .' Provocatively, Gwendolyn traces a finger down your forearm. You sense that there may be much to learn, if you follow where she leads.

Still, you can't imagine that Kannagh, her father, would be impressed at the idea of a private conversation. He runs the only inn in town, and he could be a powerful enemy.

>>> go with Gwendolyn

Gwendolyn tells you the way to her room. She bids you follow a few minutes after her, so as not to arouse suspicion.

You drink the dregs of your ale, then steal through the doorway to the kitchen and up the servants' stairs to Gwendolyn's room. You knock twice, softly, and she lets you in.

'I feared you wouldn't join me,' she says. Her hand is clutched to her chest, between her breasts which, as previously mentioned, are ample. She appears to be waiting for you to say, or do, something.

>>> kiss gwendolyn

You stride forward. Drawing Gwendolyn into your arms, you lean down and firmly seal her lips with yours. The kiss lasts for an appropriate amount of time. When you release her, Gwendolyn blushes and looks over at the bed. Things appear to be escalating quickly.

>>> hug gwendolyn

Invalid command. For instructions and a list of basic commands, type 'help'.

>>> kiss gwendolyn

You have already done that. You don't need to do that again.

>>> make love gwendolyn

Invalid command. For instructions and a list of basic commands, type 'help'.

>>> fuck gwendolyn

You remove Gwendolyn's clothes and bid her lie on the bed. Fully naked, she is even more beautiful than you had imagined. Rapidly, you achieve tumescence. You lay with her, and Gwendolyn takes you in hand, gasping in surprise at your length and girth, and guides you.

You thrust vigorously into her.

>>> eww

Invalid command. For instructions and a list of basic commands, type 'help'.

Gwendolyn moans lustily, and your movements bring her to orgasm several times in quick succession. 'charlotte!' she cries each time she climaxes.

Feeling your own peak approach, you pull out of her at the last moment and erupt, spilling your seed over her stomach and breasts.

>>> EWWW!!!

Invalid command. For instructions and a list of basic commands, type 'help'.

Immensely satisfied, Gwendolyn drifts quickly to sleep. You leave and return to the stables.

Do you want to save your game?

>>> no

Weeks pass. You continue to frequent the inn for evening ale, but you and Gwendolyn do not repeat your tryst. Once, she raises her eyebrows and indicates towards the kitchen with her eyes, but you simply return her smile and shake your head. It would not do to become too close, what with your impending departure.

Besides – Kannagh, Gwendolyn's father, seems to be scowling at you more forcefully than usual.

You save coin to outfit yourself for your coming adventure. The work is hard. One day you are careless and as you turn around, the back of your hand drags over a jagged edge sticking out from a pile of scrap. The wound is deep and leaves a scar that runs from your wrist to the base of your little finger. But you don't mind. All adventurers have scars.

Late one evening, lying on your pallet, you hear footsteps approaching. Lighting a candle, you make out Gwendolyn's lissom form as she slips inside the stable door. 'I have news,' she says. She cannot seem to meet your eyes.

When you bid her continue, she lays her hands upon her stomach. 'I am with child,' she tells you.

>>> lol

Invalid command. For instructions and a list of basic commands, type 'help'.

'Impossible!' you reply. Your knowledge of reproduction is limited to what you saw on the farm where you grew up, but you feel certain that the manner of your lovemaking should have prevented any chance of pregnancy.

'It's a miracle!' Gwendolyn says. 'Our miracle. I must tell father, of course. I'm sure that once the shock has passed he will welcome news of a grandchild.'

You are not so certain. Once Gwendolyn has told her father this news, the whole town will know. The reaction from the townsfolk is likely to be hostile. If you stay to face the consequences of your actions, it may be difficult to steal away later.

You want to do right by Gwendolyn, but perhaps the best thing for all concerned would be for you to leave now and make your fortune. Perhaps by winning some large prize. Then you would be able to return here in glory, with means to support this tavern girl and her – your – child.

What will you do? Stay or leave?

>>> stay

You settle back onto your pallet and try to rest. You'll not run.

Do you want to save your game?

>>> no

On the morrow, you are roughly shaken from sleep. When you open your eyes, Kannagh looms over you. 'Scum!' he hisses. 'You have despoiled her. My precious daughter! Mark my words: I'll see you hanged!'

You try to reason with the man, but he refuses to be calmed. By early afternoon, you have been escorted to the town priory, your arm locked in Kannagh's sturdy grip. Gwendolyn stands silently beside you. Impatient, her father moves her bodily through the ritual motions, as if she were a doll.

'By the laws of this land and the laws of all the heavens,' a morose brother intones, 'you two are now one, indivisible.' Idly, he scratches himself between his legs. 'Congratulations.'

Kannagh whips you around and clutches at your shirt. He pulls you close. 'She's yours now,' he spits. 'Do as you will. But not you, nor your new wife, nor your bastard child, will ever have aught from me.'

Gwendolyn begins to sob. You take her back to the stables. You realise that this is home, now, for both of you.

Do you want to save your game?

>>> no

The weeks pass swiftly. There is much to do. By day you continue your work at the smithy. By mutual understanding, you do not speak of your predicament to Dunn, and he does not ask questions. The rest of the townsfolk shun you.

In the evening, and with Dunn's begrudging consent, you set to work erecting a hut adjoining the stables. It will be small, and mean, but at least your new wife will have privacy and some separation from the animals. When you can work no longer, you crawl exhausted into the pallet you now share with Gwendolyn. Sometimes she stirs and you make tired love.

With lumber to buy, and a woman's needs for warmth and clothing, you find it difficult to save much coin from your work. You wonder whether you might be able to leave Gwendolyn by herself for a time, perhaps to go on a brief adventure, not too far from town. But it is impossible. Your funds would be quickly depleted if you ceased your efforts at the smithy, and Gwendolyn grows fretful if you return so much as an hour late from your work.

The seasons change. Winter is hard, and harder on your pregnant wife. You wrap her in blankets and try to patch the holes in your hut through which the draught blows. Lying together, you embrace for warmth. She seldom complains. You feel some affection for her, even as you resent the situation she has brought about.

In the spring, a son is born to you.

What will you name your firstborn?

>>> bieber

Carefully, you take your son in your arms for the first time. He is light, and warm, and he opens his eyes.

Softly, you say, 'I shall call you bieber.'

You think about all the generations that have gone before. Your parents. Their parents. Here, in a new land, you have brought about a continuation. A quiet call, coming from deep within, insists that you do all that you can for this child.

Do you want to save your game?

>>> no

Months elapse. Years. Having shouldered the burden of family – however unexpected – you mean to do what is required. Nonetheless, it is a struggle to provide for your wife and growing boy. Your labour at the smithy exhausts you. Your own sword, the one you made, grows blunt on the stable wall.

You are not welcome at the inn – indeed, you are not welcome in polite society, such as it exists in Par. But you come to know an old man in a hovel on the edge of town who makes ginger wine. In the evenings you drink this cloying brew until you fall into unconsciousness.

One day you are hammering plate with a large mallet. You are thinking about Olaf, your old horse, and not paying attention when you rest the fingers of your right hand on yellow-hot metal. You pull away quickly but you leave skin and flesh behind.

You wash and bind the index and middle fingers of your hand, but two days later pus still seeps from the wound, giving off an awful, sweet smell. You take yourself to the priory, begging the healers there to tend you. When you depart that place, you have been relieved of sixty silver pieces and two fingers from your right hand. So deprived, you will never be able to wield a sword or fire a bow.

You are not old, not yet. But you no longer call yourself an adventurer.

Do you want to save your game?

>>> no

Time passes, as time will. You try to teach your son, now five years old, some of what you have learned through bitter experience. 'Hear me, bieber. This world is cruel. It will rob you of your dreams.' But bieber only smiles. He is a happy lad for the most part, curious and gentle. He has his father's eyes and his mother's nose.

The next winter, Gwendolyn becomes gravely ill. When she coughs, her lips are flecked with red. Although her beauty has long since faded, you have grown close to her and it is hard to see her in such a state.

Once more you approach the healers at the priory, and they tell of a medicine that could alleviate the coughing. The medicine is rare and expensive: two hundred silver for a small bottle, representing almost all of the money you have saved in the years since you arrived in the village of Par.

Do you wish to purchase medicine for your sick wife?

>>> buy medicine

You give Gwendolyn a spoonful of medicine each evening, as instructed. Once more, she breathes deeply, and sleeps. But after two weeks, the colour has not returned to her face. Days after the medicine runs out, she is too weak to rise from her bed.

You sell your old sword to a tinker. It fetches a pittance, and still you cannot afford to buy more medicine. You could go begging to Gwendolyn's father, Kannagh, but he has disowned his daughter and grandson. Or, you suppose, you could try to sneak into the priory and steal more medicine for your wife. It would be almost like an adventure.

>>> steal medicine

In the pitch-black hours after midnight, you approach the priory. Levering open a side door, you sneak towards the stairwell leading to the basement that you know serves as an apothecary.

As you round a corner, you pass a score of brothers, gathered to pray. One of them spies you as you try to sneak past.

You are not a fighter. You never were. After they mete out a vicious beating, the brothers drag your limp form through town and deposit it in front of the stables.

>>> beg Kannagh

The next evening you visit the inn. You approach from the servants' entrance at the rear of the building. Kannagh is in the kitchen.

'Begone!' he shouts.

You explain that Gwendolyn is gravely ill, near death. You can see that at some level, this news grieves Kannagh. But he is a proud man. 'I told you on your wedding day: you'll have nothing from me. Now be off.'

'I have nowhere else to turn,' you cry.

'Away!'

You return home. You boil up a large pot of soup, which you feed in small sips to Gwendolyn while bieber watches on.

Her cough has returned, worse than ever, and she drools bloody saliva from the corner of her mouth.

Four days later, your wife dies in your arms.

>>> this is messed up

Invalid command. For instructions and a list of basic commands, type 'help'.

Mad with grief, you bid little bieber wait in the hut while you carry Gwendolyn, her limp body draped over your shoulder, to the river on the outskirts of town. Gently, you wash her. On a rise overlooking the riverbank, you dig a deep hole. It takes most of the day. You lower Gwendolyn's body into the hole and cover her with dirt. There is no money for a priest to say any words, so you simply say, 'Goodbye.'

That evening is your first alone with bieber. When he falls asleep, you find yourself in the company of your thoughts and a large supply of ginger wine.

>>> drink wine

You gulp down the wine, finishing the bottle quickly. The aftertaste brings tears to your eyes.

>>> drink wine

You drink another bottle of wine.

>>> drink wine

You drink another bottle of wine. It does not assuage your grief. You realise you are sobbing. bieber stirs in his bed.

>>> drink wine

You drink another bottle and find yourself prone on the floor. You are furious at the gods, at fate, at the way your life has unfolded. You were meant for other journeys. Not a son and a dead wife, not a place as a smith's apprentice. Not a hut: a horizon.

Perhaps you should sleep. Things might seem better in the morning.

>>> drink wine

You continue to drink until you lose all self-control. Fumbling, you clutch at your dagger and stuff it into the sheath at your belt. You reel outside, bearing towards the inn.

You find Kannagh in the kitchen, counting his take from the evening's trade. Coins spill from his hands when he sees you. He says something, but you can't understand. You wrap your half-hand around his neck and with your other, you draw your blade. 'She's dead,' you slur into his face.

He pleads with you to let him go.

>>> let go innkeeper

You shake your head to try to clear it, struggling for self-mastery, but you cannot let this man alone. Kannagh is scum. Your blood seethes with rage and drink. You are berserk.

>>> drop dagger

You press the blade against the innkeeper's throat.

>>> stop

You leer at the selfish bastard.

>>> stop

You press the dagger home, opening a rent in Kannagh's skin. A firm slash, and it's done. Blood gushes from Kannagh's throat and he slumps to the floor.

Do you want to save your game?

>>> FUCK no

>>> no

The next morning a small band of men, assembled from the townsfolk, arrives to take you. A trail has led them directly from Kannagh's corpse to the stables, where even now you lie caked in the blood of your dead wife's father.

bieber wails as your arms are bound with rope and you are led away.

The trial is quick and you are sentenced to hang. The magistrate explains that with no family in this land willing to take the child, and with no means of supporting himself, bieber will become a ward of the church. When he is old enough, he will be sent to work in a nearby mine. You are not permitted to see him again.

When they tie the rope around your neck, you turn to the executioner. 'I was young,' you say, imploring him to understand. 'I was strong . . .'

They hoist you up and you say nothing further.

GAME OVER – THANK YOU FOR PLAYING REALITY QUEST

Game analysis:

Monsters slain:	0 x 1000 pts	= 0 pts
Treasures found:	0 x 5000 pts	= 0 pts
Maidens rescued:	0 x 750 pts	= 0 pts
Heroic deeds:	0 x 250 pts	= 0 pts
Abandoned horse to slow death:		= (– 20 pts)
Wenches bedded:	1 x 40 pts	= 40 pts
Sons fathered:	1 x 5 pts	= 5 pts
Wife died of curable disease:		= (– 10 pts)

TOTAL SCORE: = 15 pts

You lived an unremarkable life. You did no great deeds. No-one will remember you.

Play again? Y/N

>>> n

Home Stretch

When Benji's mum came to see what the noise was about, she said there was no reason for them to be inside at all. It was the last Saturday afternoon of the Easter school break. After days of intermittent rain, the clouds had broken up and sunlight danced in the overgrown back garden.

The kids had been playing Super Nintendo, a one-player game, but there were four of them. At the start of the level, there was a jumping puzzle to navigate before you got to any bad guys. Max was five years old, and when it was his turn to play it took him ages to die. Benji suspected that his little brother was dithering to make his turn last longer, and enough was enough. He'd yanked the controller, provoking a loud whinge, and then Ella had joined in, shouting that if Max's turn was over, then it was her go. The three of them ended up in a tangle on the carpet, while Ella's brother Rory watched on, sulking.

Benji's mum wasn't interested in explanations. *Out!* she shouted. *Outside! Get some sun.* That was rich coming from her: the adults were in the dining room playing their own game, drawing pictures and yelling and drinking wine.

'Come on,' said Ella, picking herself up and throwing open the glass door to the patio. In the last year she'd grown taller. She was eleven and Benji was only ten, but still, this was Benji's place, his and Max's, and she wasn't the boss. Benji took his time, allowing the two younger kids to scoot outside, brushing chip seasoning from the crotch of his pants before he followed.

Every day was a struggle to find something new to do. Standing on the pavers, they searched the garden for a clue that would lead to fun. With autumn already arrived in the Hills, it was fresh outside, the grass still slick from a late-morning shower. The yard sloped down to a dense mess of trees at the edge of the property. Ella and Rory lived a ten-minute walk away, down a gully, along winding, shady streets without footpaths. But their house was smaller and they didn't have a Nintendo or even a Sega, so most of the time the kids hung out at Benji's place.

There was no back fence. On the other side of the trees was the railway line.

◆

Mick shifted in his seat, extending one leg and then the other, glad he'd started the slow descent through the Hills into Adelaide. He was tired and his back had started to throb a quiet warning, but it was a familiar feeling. He'd been doing the freight run from Melbourne to Adelaide for more than a decade and Mick knew every bend along the line, but this stretch was his favourite. He wasn't impatient about the crawl the engine was reduced to by tight turns and the slope. Past the top of the range everything turned green, or at least greener than anything since Bordertown.

◆

A couple of years ago, Benji's dad had looped a swing over the branch of an old ginkgo tree. Really it was just two bits of rope supporting a plank. The summer before last it had been terrifying, the way you drew it back up the hill to get on, and then as it rocked forward the ground fell away. But too many afternoons had passed, and now it was lame. On a dull day the week before, Benji and Max had dared each other to let go at the farthest point of the arc, but neither child had the courage.

So while Rory ran to the swing and took off – it was still a novelty for him – the others milled around the edge of the garden, kicking at the large grey mushrooms that seemed to spring up each night.

'Dare you to eat one,' said Ella.

'Dare *you*,' Benji fired back lazily. He and Ella had spent too long together, and both had a sense of what the other would and wouldn't do.

Ella said, 'Hey Max, you do it. I'll pay you twenty cents.'

Max was easily bought. Ever since he'd started school and his parents had opened him a savings account, he'd been on the lookout for coins. He'd become a master at extracting change from the back of the lounge. Max took the mushroom in his small hand, sniffed it inquisitively. He was a chubby kid, and one of his eyelids drooped a bit, making him look sleepy.

Rory came running over. 'Don't! That's *poison*!'

Ella rolled her eyes. 'Don't be a baby. The grey ones are fine.'

'I'm not!' Rory whined. 'If you eat mushrooms off the ground you get poison and die.'

Max looked from face to face with a dumb half-smile, seemingly content to let the others decide. Benji thought Ella was probably right, it was probably fine, but still. His parents had told him what it meant to be a big brother. It meant he had to look out for Max. Especially Max: Mum said the younger boy was *credulous*. Benji had needed to look that up in the dictionary.

He smashed his hand over Max's fist, and the mushroom disintegrated.

◆

Mick had killed two people. At the training sessions they talked about *Track Obstruction Events*, but killing was how he thought about it when he was alone.

The first had been after midnight just out from Keith, and he hadn't even known until head office rang him the next day, after he'd finished his shift. That one wasn't so bad. For sure, it had played on his mind, and in the week after, his ex-wife – this was back when they were still married – said he'd been quiet. But there was nothing anyone could do. It didn't seem worth getting into with her.

The next one was worse. Late morning, on an isolated stretch between Stawell and Horsham. He'd had enough time to take it all in. Enough time for his hand to reach for the emergency brake, before he realised it was no good. They were doing a hundred and five on the flat. Loaded as it was, the train he was driving could decelerate at no more than three ks an hour every second. Trying to brake any harder was worse than pointless. The wheels would lock up and it'd take even longer to stop.

He'd found out later that the victim was seventeen. His car, an old Datsun, was parked off to the side. He was still, laid on his back across the tracks, head turned to face what was coming, mouth wide. There was a sound like a boot hitting a wooden door. Hardly a jolt at all – Mick might even have imagined the feeling. But that thudding sound still woke him up some nights.

Procedure was to radio in, describe the incident and its location. The police were called, had a standard list of questions, but everyone understood that these things happened.

◆

There was nothing for the children in the garden, so they drifted lower and lower, hanging from the branches of the trees at the bottom of the yard, pelting acorns at each other.

'I wish I could fly,' said Rory.

'I had a dream last night that I saw an angel,' said Max.

Ella said, 'By the year two thousand, some people will be flying little planes to get to work. It was on the news.'

'That's stupid,' said Benji.

Ella was the first to break through to the clearing on the other side. The tracks here cut a gentle curve as they rounded back gardens on both sides of the line. Mostly, people had planted trees to dull the noise, so you couldn't see the houses from the tracks. The corridor felt like its own place, secluded and silent. It was mainly goods trains that came along here, two or three a day. On the side opposite Benji's place there was a path leading down to a little creek, and the kids were allowed to hop the tracks and play there, so long as they were careful when they crossed. *Don't muck around*, Benji's dad always said. *Listen for the train. You'll hear it before you see it.*

Benji and Max knew vaguely when the trains ran. If it hadn't passed already, Benji reckoned one shouldn't be far away. Even though they weren't supposed to loiter here, they often did. One day Benji had put a fifty-cent piece on the track because another kid told him it'd be squashed flat after the train was gone. Benji and Max had waited in the trees as it crawled by. Benji had tried running alongside, as fast as he could on the uneven gravel that flanked the sleepers, but it had easily outpaced him. It only *looked* slow. When they went back for the coin, they couldn't find it.

◆

When he got to Adelaide, there wouldn't be much waiting for Mick. He'd get a taxi to a budget motel in the suburbs where the drivers were put up. The next morning there was a roster change, so he'd fly back to Melbourne rather than hang around for a crew job on the return journey. If they'd been in his position, with nothing to do the following day, he knew most of the other drivers would head to the city. If you went looking for trouble you usually found it, but Mick was trying to be better than that. His daughter, Chrissy, was growing up, in primary school now. When they spent time together, he could tell that she'd started paying attention to the kind of man he was. Chrissy needed at least one positive male influence in her life, and God knows, her mother's new boyfriend was a deadshit.

There was a good Chinese takeaway across the road from

the motel. He'd go there, place an order. Wander over to the servo and buy some magazines, have a night to himself.

◆

Ella was drop-kicking rocks. She looked bored, and that made Benji angry, but he didn't know why.

'Have you ever played train dance?' he asked her.

She shook her head. 'What's that?'

Benji laughed, stalling. 'Don't you know? Oh my God.' He wished he'd come up with a better name. 'It's where you . . . stand on the train line, and then the train comes, and the last person to move is the winner.'

'Sounds dumb.'

'Are you scared? *Now* who's a baby?' Benji bunched his hands into fists and jammed them against his eyes. 'Waah! Waah!'

Ella sighed theatrically. 'Whatever.' She turned to study him. 'How can you both be on the tracks at the same time? Wouldn't you get in each other's way?'

'Nah, you – one person stands in front, and then the next person stands, like, twenty metres behind, and then the next person . . . so that everyone has time to watch everyone.'

'Okay,' said Ella. 'Well, since you've played before, you stand in front.' She motioned towards a sleeper. Even now she was trying to boss him around, tell him where to be, even though it was his game.

'Fine,' he said, stepping over the rail. 'You go back there. Further . . . further . . . that's good.'

From off to the side, over near the trees, Rory shouted, 'What are you doing?' He and Max were crouched down over something Benji couldn't see.

'Nothing,' Ella shouted back. 'Just stay there, okay? Benji and I are trying a thing.'

◆

Mick kept an easy pressure on the brake. Guidelines were to stay at thirty ks an hour through this section, and there was no point rushing.

He knew this stretch well. He was slicing through the back-streets of Stirling, and after this gentle right-hander, the track would bend the other way, passing by the old, disused Mount Lofty platform.

The kids were standing so still that it took Mick a moment to spot them. And then another split-second to register – standing on the tracks one in front of the other, a carriage-length apart, legs planted wide in an A-shape, like the entrance and exit to an invisible tunnel.

'Jesus.' Children playing on the tracks was nothing new, but something about the way the closest one looked up at him made his chest tight. A boy, and his scowl was feral.

Mick gave the horn a blast.

◆

An air horn sounded from the train, and it was so loud that Benji flinched despite himself. He could see the engine and the first few cars around the side of the hill now. The train had its lights on but they were feeble in the afternoon sun. The engine was huge, taller than Benji remembered, and as it got closer it came at him fast.

He had to stay on the tracks until the very last second. He had to show Ella that he wasn't chicken. He wanted to turn around and look for her, but the train was almost on him now and it was too late to do anything but wait, get the timing right.

◆

'Get off, you little shit.' Mick smacked his hand against the windshield. 'Get off. GET OFF.'

◆

Benji stuck fast until the last moment – and then a split second longer – and then he jumped high and long to his right, clearing the rail and the sleepers. Even as he did so, he looked behind. Ella was on the other side of the tracks, halfway to the trees, pointing and laughing at him. She had faked him out, he realised – she'd never intended to play his game. But that wasn't what made him turn so fast he stumbled.

Beyond Ella, Max had taken up a position on the line.

Benji started running, but the train was almost level with him now, and moving faster. 'Ella!' he screamed, pointing past her, and she wheeled around to look.

◆

Mick watched the first kid clear the tracks, just before he would've been lost to view beneath the windshield. Okay. But the next one, he was just a little tacker. He looked comfortable, distracted, not focused like the older boy. Something about the way his head kept moving, never looking straight ahead, gave Mick a chill. It was too late already, but he pressed harder on the brake.

◆

On the other side of the tracks, Ella spotted Max, started bolting up the line towards him.

'Max!' Benji screamed. 'Move!' His little brother looked up, calm expression turning confused. His head jagged right and left, like he couldn't decide which way he should jump.

Ella was running fast, but as Benji watched, the train caught up, blocked his view of her. The front of the engine moved past him, and the metal grind of the wheels was all he could hear. Now Max looked worried, but he hadn't shifted. The boy raised one foot, like he didn't know what it was for.

◆

A girl – there was a girl off to the right, sprinting for the kid. The little kid who still hadn't moved. Mick had the brakes on tight. Too tight? He was braced, frozen. He couldn't have eased up if he'd wanted to.

The kid wasn't moving, he looked terrified, and the girl was running, and she dropped from view under the rim of the windshield. She was close—

And now the kid was below him—

And then he was past, and he didn't know. Mick didn't know.

◆

Benji ran, tears streaming. The train was slowing down, but by now the engine and the first carriage were well beyond where Max had been standing.

Benji dropped to his knees, trying to look under the cars as they rolled by, slower and slower. And he could see – he could make out a bundle on the ground – Ella in her pink T-shirt, and the green of Max's shorts. Nothing moved but the train.

A sound behind him – Rory was wailing, he had seen it all. 'Did she get him?' Benji asked the boy. Rory turned away, bolted into the trees back towards the house.

It took a long minute for the train to stop. Benji crawled under a coupling where two cars met. He found Ella cradling Max's head in her lap. Max was looking up at her, mute. But all of him was there.

Benji knelt alongside. He punched his brother's arm as hard as he could. 'You idiot! Why didn't you jump!? I thought—'

He couldn't finish the sentence. Wet trails ran in parallel lines down his face. Pitching forward, stones dug into the flesh of his palms.

The children stayed like that until the driver got to them, red and out of breath.

A breeze stirred the trees, sending a rustling down the corridor. Benji glanced up, caught a look from the driver, who was standing, hands on hips, like he'd run a race. More than anything he seemed sad, and Ella did too. Max stared up at the sky, maybe watching a cloud, or thinking about something else, his face a study in tranquillity. Eyes half-closed like he might drift off. And it was fine. If Benji could just explain before the recriminations started, he would remind them – his parents, the driver, Max – that everyone was well, and everyone was accounted for.

Camelopard

Most of the time, I know I'm human. There's a buttoned flap to fuss with when it's time to eat, and another for the toilet. Every enhancement comes at a price.

It's not good teamwork to complain, not when things are going so well. Seven games in and the men are winning more often than not. And our girls – females – *women* – are top of the table. Boss tells me the crowds are down a little on last year, but that's hard to notice at game time, as I'm cantering along the boundary, sidestepping photographers and guards, rearing and paddling my forelegs.

Stampede! the announcer booms through the PA. Fans jab their fists at the empty air and shout, '*raffes! 'raffes! 'raffes!*'

It's the most a creature can feel. Later, once the players have jogged down the tunnel and the punters have filtered out, I will watch the cleaning crew shove cups into plastic bags as they move through the bays. I'll mooch, and scrape my hoof-hands against the mottled fur covering my belly, and wait for the massive towers set at each corner of the ground to surrender the sky. If I close my eyes for a minute or two, the afterimages of those terrible bulbs will fade and a subtler gradient will reveal itself. Before I settle, before I can even think of turning in for the night, I will trace slow laps around the perimeter. To make sure everything is safe.

◆

It's evening on a not-weekend and the light is on in Boss's office, so I hover in the doorway. Before long he clicks his tongue. I trot in and kneel next to him on the floor. In that position, my long neck protrudes above the desk, and he leans forward and rubs the snout of my suit-head affectionately. 'There's my big fella. There you go, mate,' he coos as he rubs.

Long ago, Boss used to play the game. He was a hero in his day, but he has grown too wide and deep. His heavy head is soft at the edges, like the full bags of sand the ground staff carry on their carts. Boss now turns his tactical mind to spreadsheets, marketing plans, everything that can hold our organisation together. His gigantic forehead crinkles when he reads, and his short, sandy-grey hair is patchy, like the fuzz on my rump.

I don't feel the way he strokes me like I'd feel someone touching my old-skin. But where he rests his hand, there's a pressure that translates as a tugging sensation, and it comforts just the same.

Boss makes sure I have everything I need. Time is hazy, but when I relocated to the stadium, I remember that all my things fit into a sturdy plastic shopping bag, the kind they hand out at department stores. Boss found me the suit and a silent place to sleep: a disused janitor's closet with blankets and a radio with big buttons that I can manipulate with my hoofs. When something sticky lodges in my pelt, he takes cloth and dishwashing detergent and rubs in gentle circles till I'm almost good as new. He makes sure the catering entrance to the northwest kiosk is left ajar so that I can help myself to water and whatever else is left there between events.

Our stadium is flanked by a settlement that is either a large town or a small city. From the top of the main stand, you can look north and see the plains fold upward. Beyond the hills, obscured by haze most days, there are mountains. This is something I remember from before. In the mountains, horses roam free.

'It'll be a hard run home,' Boss says to me, still stroking, looking up and past my head to the framed jerseys hanging on the wall. 'For the competition. For us.'

I snort and wriggle, and he says, 'Don't worry. We're a team. We look after each other.'

Solace can be found in strange places – I don't deny it.

◆

My giraffe body protects me from pretty much everything, and that's one of the reasons I enjoy it. Children are always sneaking up and pulling my tail, and over the seasons it has frayed badly, but it doesn't ache. Kids and men jostle me or punch my stomach, but with all the padding I am usually safe.

The next game day, twenty minutes before kick-off, I make my way to the mezzanine. The roof of the main grandstand curves disapprovingly, like an upper lip, and the storerooms underground are the lower lip or maybe the jowls, but either way that makes the mezzanine the straight line where the incisors meet. It's where Izzy parks his baked-potato cart.

I ask for one with The Lot because I love the way the sour cream and cheese melt over the potato, and the bacon pieces

cluster in the centre of the cross-cut, waiting for my long tongue
to reach down and curl them up. Iskender gives me a free spud
every game, as long as I eat in front of him. He says that Jerry
Giraffe eating a baked potato is the highlight of his week. Today
there are spectators milling, trying to find the right gap in the
teeth so they can take their seats, and they suspend their conversations and watch, too. When I lick the bottom of the box
clean and hold it up for inspection, they cheer.

What Izzy does makes me happy, and it seems that I make
him happy too, and that means we are friends. But at kick-off
my abdomen hurts, and by first drinks I have lost my easy gallop.

Even though my own performance is substandard, this is
not enough to hold up the match. Half-time break is called
and the field is emptied. There are meant to be bollards and
tape lining the players' race to keep the fans at a distance, but
today there are no bollards. A man leans over the edge of the
ramped bank of seats adjacent to the race. He grabs the collar of one of our wingers, draws him close and runs his tongue
up the player's jaw and over his ear, collecting the sweat. This
is not right, our young man is just here to play football, there
are no standards anymore. When I see things like this, I worry
that there is no sanctuary.

◆

At sleep time, I shut my eyes tight before I take my head off.
After so long looking through the gauze of my suit's neck-hole,
it can be jarring to see the world directly. The air settles cold
on my naked forehead, so I burrow under my blanket, just like

a calf's head seeks the warm space near its mother's loin. I feel ashamed. I might not be a player, but I am a mascot, and that means that I am a symbol of the team. Even though (I keep telling myself) I am not really a giraffe, I am the next best thing for many days' walk in any direction.

In the dark, I can't help but remember certain events, and tonight, it's the end-of-season party for the women's comp two seasons ago. The girls dragged me into their huddle and spun me round. They'd reached the semis before losing to their arch-rivals, and that night there was a strange, thwarted energy to the proceedings. They sung the team song and stroked the fur between my legs and emptied bottles of beer over me. For the most part I am damp-resistant, but a bit sloshed in through my face-hole and ran down my neck and back, and pooled in my hoofs. Beer was all I could smell.

When the party was over, Boss handed me a roll of paper towel and I dabbed sheets against my coat until they turned soggy. That night I slept with my legs off, which I hate to do unless it can't be helped.

◆

Saturday rolls round like it always does. Only this time, Izzy can't give me one with The Lot. Because of shortages, he says, sour cream and bacon have become hard to get. As a substitute, he does me a Mexican (no guacamole, also due to shortages), and he looks upset even though he hasn't done anything wrong.

A couple of fans stroll by and sneak glances, but they don't loiter. I finish up the potato, and even though I don't like it as much as The Lot, I hold up the empty box and whicker my approval.

A prayer is an appeal to a higher power, and that being the case, I've spent almost my whole life in prayer. As a boy in various institutions. As a valueless man. Here, I don't need to ask for anything. I labour, and I get what I get, and it's plenty.

'It's not a good time to be alone,' Iskender says.

◆

Something is happening in the town. I have shucked my outer skin and stolen away from the stadium in the middle of the night, dressed in team apparel borrowed from the merchandising stand. I've also taken some notes from the petty-cash box in the finance office (they keep the key in the bottom drawer of the filing cabinet) and I wonder if anyone will notice, but they never have before.

I do this once a season. It is mostly alarming and not enjoyable at all, but it helps to remind me what I was. Boss doesn't know, and I'm not sure how he'd feel about it, but anyway there is no regulation that would prevent me from coming and going as I please.

Once I would have understood fully, but now I can only trust what I sense. The city smells like danger, like decomposition, but I am a free man tonight, so I can't turn back.

I head to an entertainment district that feels familiar. I believe I knew it well. A man runs up to me in front of a convenience store and tugs at my team shirt and holds his hands in front of his face, palms forward. It's not a gesture of submission;

he wants me to slap them as a demonstration of our shared love of the team. I turn a corner, but the street lights are out and groups of young people are sat on the pavement, so I feel funny about going any further in that direction. Instead, I spot a bar across the street and walk as briskly towards it as my two legs will carry me. Inside, I point to a fridge, at a bottle of pre-mixed rum and Coke, fumblingly passing over too many plastic notes. The room is small and raucous, and the sugar in the drink quickly makes me agitated. This is what being human is like in a town, and long ago I might have enjoyed it, but now I believe I have had enough and I leave through the front door and run home before someone tries to fight me.

◆

Two games later, there aren't enough patrons to fill the inner bowl of seats ringing the park. The steps to both grandstands are gated and locked, which makes me angry because I like to sit up high in the evenings and watch the sun drop onto the land like an egg yolk on a plate of rice.

It's harder to work when the crowd is subdued. I pump my fists and run and do a flying kick in the air, but inside the humid atmosphere of my head, all I can hear is my own breathing.

The competitors must feel it too. Returning to the change-rooms at half-time, they move in a tight pack, taking care not to stray too close to the walls of the race. A group of the older players are being rested, which isn't too strange at this point in the regular competition, but they haven't even come to the game. I keep my ears open, but I don't hear anything about injuries.

Mostly the chatter from the sidelines is about banks and a withdrawal freeze that's making people worried about their savings. I wonder if I should be worried, too. Boss says he's invested my salary (after living expenses and taxes) in a term deposit.

Our boys lose to a side they would normally dismantle. Afterwards, Boss takes to the field and, speaking through a microphone gripped in his big fist, thanks the fans for their loyalty in these difficult times. 'I truly believe that sport can help us heal the divisions we face each day, outside this place. Go well, be safe, and we hope to see you again in two weeks, when our beloved 'raffes take on the Lobsters. All going to plan, kick-off will be at four.'

◆

In the off-seasons, I am called on less frequently. Boss sometimes loads me into the back of his SUV and we roll across to a private residence where a child is having a birthday party. I prance and pose for photos. There have been occasional fund-raising dinners and promotional events where I am expected to wave as the guests arrive and then remove myself as the entrees are served. After Christmas there is usually a junior coaching clinic. And the stadium is used for cricket in the summer. I don't like cricketers at all, but I stay out of their way, and they usually stay out of mine.

In the hills, wild horses eat grass, fruits, the leaves of small bushes, insects, kitchen scraps. They go wherever they want and if there's anything they don't like, they trample it until it's crushed in the dirt.

◆

Boss has summoned me to his office. It's been weeks since we've spoken outside of game times. The big screen, mounted on the wall opposite his desk, shows horses being led around a yard. Their coats are so lustrous, they seem to shimmer as their muscles shift. He asks me if I recognise any cousins. Says there's a big race about to start. He's moving restlessly, and there are plenty of used bottles lined up by the wall. As I walk in, papers stacked high on his desk slide to the floor, like those clifftop houses they showed on the news, but Boss doesn't care.

The horses are led into slots behind a barrier and I see them toss their heads. And then the gates open and they bolt, and my breath gets stuck in my chest as I comprehend their power and speed. The thumping sound as their hoofs strike the turf presses on something under my suit, under the old-skin.

But then, one of those horses breaks down at the end of the first turn. It's in the corner of the frame, and the camera pans and it's lost from view. My mind replays the moment where the fetlock snaps.

'Poor bastard.' Boss lets out a chuckle, but when he turns and looks at me, his mouth tightens into a grimace. Although I am still and my face is the usual length, Boss is very percept-ive. 'Won't suffer long,' he says gruffly.

After the race is over, Boss gets me down on all fours and he slides himself until his bottom rests in the dip between my rib cage and my coccyx. He pretends to whip me and I bear him slowly around the room. The weight of him is scarcely tolerable, but I don't falter. My legs, my back: it turns out they are strong.

I want to say, *Thanks for everything you've done*, and I also very much wish he would hop off. But I'm not Mister Ed, I'm just a giraffe, so I say nothing.

◆

Another Saturday morning, but I'm not seeing the crews who usually arrive to get things ready. With an hour to go until kick-off, the front gates are still locked. At go time, the team captains and the referee huddle by the sidelines. It seems the visitors are three men short of a full complement, and so our boys agree to play two down, and one of our reserves is loaned to the other side so that the game can proceed.

There's a knot of people up by the fence near the players' benches. Two coaches, a drinks runner, a medic, the ref and a few spectators who have managed to turn out despite everything. They stand silently, looking at the empty field so they don't have to look at one another. Most of them wear backpacks. Some carry knives slung through belt loops. Others keep cricket bats or makeshift clubs within easy reach. These are the true fans, and I recognise most of their faces. I trot over, but Boss sees me coming and shakes his head.

I watch the game from the top of the eastern stand, which is accessible again now that the padlock on the security gate is busted. The players look small from up here. It's quiet, and my gaze drifts past the on-field action, past the edge of the western concourse, above the ramped earth and the trees, to the centre of town. A grubby trail of smoke is rising above the business district. I can see cars unmoving on the highway, and if the roads are blocked, maybe that explains the poor turn-out. Boss will be disappointed with ticket sales. The game is decided by a penalty.

◆

I miss Izzy most of all. He was my good friend. Boss looked out for me, but I've decided he was never my friend. If he had been, he wouldn't have left without a goodbye.

It's been days and days since the last game. How many, exactly? I couldn't tell you. I am an even-toed ungulate. We can't count past eight, and it's been more days than that.

For a while, the streets around the stadium were loud, but now they are not. There has been no football, and no talk of football. The power has gone out, and I'm glad. There is no light at all in the service tunnels, and no-one except me knows the way to my sleeping closet.

At first I ate too much from the canteen, before I realised that stocks were low. Now I need to ration chip packets and stiff bread rolls. There are plenty of soft drinks left. I won't starve anytime soon.

There has never been so much time and space in which to canter. I try to shout, but it seems I have lost my voice, and the best I can manage is a kind of rusty honk.

◆

The machine inside that works the limbs is growing weak. But that's not what matters. A breeze plays over my fur. Just because

I can't feel the wind doesn't mean it's not there. It means I'm more than I was.

I've been learning to graze on the turf of the main playing surface. It is special ground, and in normal times this behaviour would be wrong. But no-one has been here to water it for a long time, and weeds are sprouting at the southern end. If I can learn to live off what the ground provides, then it will tether me to this place now that Boss, the players, Izzy – everyone's gone. But it isn't easy: if I take more than a few mouthfuls at a time, my old stomach gets cross, and yellow-green puke splashes the concrete beneath the visitors' benches, where I sit with my neck between my knees.

◆

Now that I am alone, I am remembering facts and key moments. I know I have been a human, and it's not that I want anything different. But what's happening is happening. It seems like many are struggling in these difficult times.

When I was at St Christopher's, after I was kicked off the Alternative Accommodation Scheme, I got treated pretty much as I deserved. I sold myself to Boss for a pouch of Eternal Red and the promise of a quiet place to sleep. Later, he explained what I would have to become.

People are cruel and weak. That is two ways of saying the same thing. Giraffes, horses, zebras – all herbivorous mammals of the plains and hills – we are more resilient. I have trained my body to ruminate on fibres. What I eat still comes back up, but I feel that I am taking in ample nutrients to sustain my activities.

Not too long ago, I had a team. I represented them. The team meant everything. I gave it everything, and I believed it was everything. But when times got hard, the team didn't look after me, and in fact there was no team. No-one is coming to tend me. I have had many, many, many days alone, but it's only now that the thoughts join up in a simple line.

This isn't my home anymore.

And: I know where it must be.

I climb the perimeter fence. This is not easy, not what I was built for, but now that I have a plan I am determined.

I trot down a ruined street, aimed north to the mountains, and my tongue knocks like a wet heart against the roof of its enclosure. *Kah-klok, kah-klok, kah-klok, kah-klok, kah-klok.*

A Straight Line

The end (part 1)

One night in late autumn it's eleven thirty before he finds a way past the billboards, the sewer grates and the cyclists; a way to satisfy the complex system he's invented to ascribe numerical values to street names. Isaac feels victorious. More and more often now, he is failing. The city has turned against him, using rain and rotting leaves to block him when cars and concrete and humans can't do the job.

Jess is at her desk – she is always at her desk – and she turns her chair at the sound of the lock.

She studies him. 'Isaac . . .' She must be trying to stay calm. She takes a breath, and he notices the darkness under her eyes. He doesn't remember her looking like that, but it's difficult to remember what someone really looked like months or years ago.

Another shallow inhalation. 'Is it just that you don't care?' She says it slowly, but there is a little tremor. Yes. Isaac can hear it: a quick oscillation in pitch as she asks the question. It signifies emotion. The pupils in her eyes are full pools.

There must exist a set, a sequence, that could lay everything out plain: words to conjure a diagram of his love and worry. There would be enough truth there to make her comprehend. But he can't find what he needs. She's the one who's good with words.

'Why won't you tell me? Why don't you come home?'

Sometimes, the only way to make things clear is to rearrange the story. Panicking, he pulls at her hand. Because she has to know, she lets him lead.

4.

Their living room was on the first floor. Glass windows faced the street, traffic obscured by the canopy of a large plane tree, grown up from the dirt between the footpath and the road. In the spring, rainbow lorikeets claimed the best spots, hanging inverted and swivelling their heads to pick at the brown pods dangling from the ends of the thinnest branches.

Isaac's gaze flicked between the tree and their TV cabinet, varnished pine, set against the far wall.

Tree --> timber.

You could stare at wood grain for hours and still not understand it, how it had formed; each plank a topography, a fragment carved from a larger puzzle.

On their sideboard, Jess kept photographs in frames. Photos with her friends; of Jess with a beloved great-aunt, a librarian. Dead now. A picture of Jess and Isaac. At her insistence, there was an image of him alone, looking down the barrel of the camera, lips parted as if he were about to object. If it had been up to him, Isaac would have put the photos in a drawer, but Jess's instincts were better. He didn't resent that – he knew that he required her. She would call him back in, gently, when he strayed too far from the world. But now she was the one who needed a guide. He was trying his hardest, but she wasn't listening.

3.

When they'd been living together for almost a year, Jess landed a job in state politics. Her new boss was an up-and-comer; tipped to be finance minister if his side got back in at the next election. Doing media for the local council had kept her busy, but now work found its way into every crack of idle time. She told Isaac it was thrilling.

In the evenings, while she watched from their couch, Isaac used to pour out measures from the box of wine in their fridge. But now Jess had to give that up, in case she was asked to draft something. She often did get requests late at night: a few paragraphs would be needed for a speech, or talking points for a radio interview. *The Shadow Minister said that the Government's job creation and investment policies were a dog's breakfast. 'Small businesses are feeling the squeeze from higher power bills, and still this mob does nothing.'*

In the mornings, she would get up well before Isaac, slip on tracksuit pants and a cardigan, and scan the newspapers.

10.

Afterwards, when Isaac was unloading the dishwasher, she pressed him. 'Why were you so late on Tuesday?'

He put down the cutlery tray. There was no way out; he said, 'Most of the suppliers have been identified. We were reviewing bank transfers. There were some questionable entries, and—'

'I was talking to Phil. He saw you over on Tarrant Street.'

There had to be a way to explain himself. Every day he worked, and every night the city was remade. He could almost sketch it out, but the edges were unclear and every time he moved closer to what he wanted to say, he was diverted along some tangent. 'I was walking.'

'That's what Phil said. Over on the other side of town.'

'I was coming home. I was trying to come home.'

'You weren't trying very hard.'

They didn't speak about it after that. They didn't speak much at all. On the weekends, he would work and she would work and sometimes they would watch television. They would sit together quietly and read. They would share meals. But they didn't make love, and they didn't discuss what might be wrong with her, or what was wrong with him.

The end (part 3)

'We'll do it together,' he says.

They start back towards their apartment, but at the next set of lights they have to turn left to fall in behind an old man walking by himself. Isaac lets Jess choose their direction at the corner, but stops her when she tries to lead them down Mendel Street.

'It's a game. A maze,' Jess says.

'It's the way home.'

It takes them an hour to find a solution. It's a cool night and she shivers. He puts his arm around her waist and they pair their steps.

At their front door, Jess pulls back. 'What happens now?'

'We've finished,' he replies. 'We reached—'

'. . . The end.'

'The end.'

Inside, the hallway is warm, and Isaac can tell that the heater has been left on.

Start again

After Jess moved in, Isaac made sure to arrive home at a reasonable hour. It was a twenty-five-minute walk, as the streets ran, from his office to their apartment. And the streets ran straight: a city isn't a maze.

It didn't take long for routines to develop. They shopped for furniture. They cooked. The first, fast heartbeat of adult work impelled them, and at night they sat side by side at their small dinner table, Jess clacking away on her laptop, Isaac contemplating a spreadsheet. He was a forensic accountant, a report-writer. He spent most of his days tracing failed businesses, unwinding asset transfers.

Jess nudged him with her shoulder. 'I need something for a Twitter announcement. The council's closing the Francis Street Dog Park. Just for the weekend – so they can plant some trees.'

Isaac didn't look up, but he released the page he'd been reading and it settled on the pile in front of him. 'Dogs are friendly,' he said. 'Domesticated. The relationship between dog and owner is usually good for the owner, and good for the dog. Exercise is a need. A park can be the site of play and exercise. Recreational spaces are well-loved and can foster a sense of community.' He stopped to consider what might come next.

'Never mind.' She squeezed his leg. 'There's a character limit.'

9.

Sitting still, his brain felt inert. A preserved specimen of a mind, suspended in formaldehyde, just as a varnished TV cabinet is a specimen of a tree. While he moved, at least his brain had a body, and his body had a purpose. He was trying to help her.

Was the failure hers or his? It was intractable.

5.

'I've told you about Susan, haven't I? Our office manager? Older lady?'

'You like her.' Isaac was preparing dinner.

'I . . . Yeah, I like her. Except, after it happened, she went to pick up something from the printer, and she wouldn't look me in the eye for the rest of the afternoon.'

Isaac frowned. He used the flat of his knife to scrape all the shredded carrot into a pile in the middle of the chopping board, pressing on the sides to make a square. Isaac was doing most of the cooking now. The other day, Jess's mother had popped in, uninvited, to vacuum, and had casually mentioned to Isaac that she'd be happy to call by each week, just to keep things tidy. *While you're both struggling.* Jess didn't seem troubled by this intervention, but Isaac found it humiliating. He said, 'Tell me again.'

Jess leaned forward on her stool, watching him use the knife. 'I stuffed up. My release about incentives for first home buyers. I thought I got it right, but I didn't really understand the effect of the stamp duty concessions. I could have checked—'

'There was a deadline.'

'Yes. There was a deadline. So I sent it for approval. And then this afternoon, at my desk, I could tell someone was standing behind me.' Her back tensed as she remembered the feeling. 'It was him. He had a copy of the draft. I'm not sure if he meant to toss it *at* me, but anyway I kind of flinched and it landed on my keyboard. He said, *Sloppy work from a sloppy girl.* The whole office heard.

'I guess I was just staring at him, but – this is what I can't figure out – before he walked off, he *winked* at me. I hope— ... I hope it was his way of saying that there are no hard feelings.'

'He shouldn't have winked at you. It's too unclear.'

She moved around the counter to where Isaac was standing and took his shoulders in her hands, shaking him in mock frustration. She smiled, but he could see that it wasn't a real smile. 'Six weeks in, and I've blown it. He won't trust me now.'

It was time to serve, and he brought the pan over from the stove. 'You're whole,' he reminded her. 'What you were before is still what you are.' She nodded and bent down to get two plates out of the cupboard.

But the following night he came home to find her sobbing, hunched over a discussion paper about water trading. 'How am I supposed to understand this?'

'Stop,' he said. He said it gently, and he meant: *stop working; give it a break for a while.* She blew her nose and kept reading, pausing every now and then to wipe away tears. When he went to bed, she was still reading.

8.

The sun began to slip between buildings. After twelve hours of reconciliations, Isaac passed between the sliding glass doors of his office and stood on the footpath, blinking. A haze had settled over the city and the air smelled of wood smoke.

A knowledge caught at Isaac's mind. It didn't seem to have an origin. There was no justification, and no scope for doubt: if anyone carrying a shopping bag crossed his path, he would need to stop and wait for thirty seconds.

Isaac tacked up a lane running parallel to the pedestrian mall, crossing through jammed lines of cars and back again to avoid this penalty. The structures and the sky had dressed for business, adopting a palette of grey and navy blue. In his suit, in the smoke, he was almost invisible.

Later the same week, street numbers between twenty and sixty were off limits. It took a wide circumvention and a zig-zag to reach their apartment, but he found his way.

Isaac didn't spend any time formulating these puzzles. At the end of his workday they were either waiting for him – or not. But increasingly, there were strictures; codes he would adopt and then discard at the end of his commute. When he managed to find a way through, he would arrive in good spirits, ready to do everything he could. Sometimes it was beyond him. One humid night he spent three hours trying to find a route absent of pubs and coffee shops, post offices and fire hydrants, before he had to admit defeat. He had no patience for Jess then. At the first opportunity, when she looked wearily at him and grumbled, he squeezed her hand. 'You're upset. Your unhappiness has a cause. Deal with the cause.'

'There's nothing I can do.'

That was false: to his ear, patently so. He could tell her to grow up, but Isaac understood enough by now to wonder. She was snarled inside. What if she really believed that there was no way to make things easier?

Jess turned to face her computer, probably tired of watching him think. 'Let's get takeaway tonight,' she said to her screen. He nodded and found the shelf where they kept the menus. It was good that she wanted to eat something substantial. He'd been arriving home to find her nibbling on chips or stale cake as she typed, her appetite ruined.

He imagined what it would be like to deliver pizza. *A city is a system for the efficient movement of people and goods. Dead-ends are rare, arising from planning failures and accidents of history.* What could be more satisfying than bringing someone a meal?

When she came to bed that night he was dozing. He roused himself and tried to find some words. But when he forced them out, they brought no relief, for her or for him. 'Your hair – black – it makes a perfect frame. Your face ... is the sort of face I could cherish.'

She murmured an acknowledgement, her mind elsewhere.

11.

When she looked at him now, he could only wait. She released her suspicion in waves, like something unstable, decaying. 'It's after nine,' she said as he shut the front door.

He shrugged. 'So many transactions. A failing business buys and sells until the last day. Sometimes after the last day.' He concentrated on unlacing his shoes, ignoring the tightness in his guts. He wasn't good at explaining himself. Since they'd started together, he had tried to be honest. But now, from the moment he came home, he was forced into evasions and half-truths.

Dinner that night was grim. He cooked the steaks too long, and their attempts at conversation failed. When he stood to start clearing up the plates, she said, 'That afternoon at the gallery. Do you know why I asked you to grab a coffee with me?'

He remembered the day. Jess had been helping with an exhibition for local artists sponsored by the council. Isaac returned two days in a row, on his lunch break, to stare at one particular painting: abstract curls of green and blue that suggested an estuary.

'I watched you for a while,' Jess said, 'before I came up. You had this expression, like someone was showing you the secrets of the universe. When I asked what was so interesting, you said, *There's so much to understand.* And then you looked at me the same way you'd looked at that painting. Guileless, fascinated. And I felt like I knew everything about you.'

He took a step towards her, wracking his mind for something to say, but she spoke again. 'When you look at me like that, I don't feel like such a failure. But it's not enough.'

He started to reach for her. He hesitated, his hand outstretched.

'I don't need you to fix me – that's not your job. But you need to show me that you get it.'

7.

The next time she got a break, a rare night away from her phone, Isaac seized the opportunity. He took her to see *Ghostbusters*.

It was a remake of an older movie. Four women were trying to fight ghosts, but it was difficult, because even though the ghosts were real, no-one would believe them. There was a dumb joke about a dog called *Mike Hat*, and Jess and Isaac both laughed, caught each other laughing, and clasped hands over the armrest.

Coming out of the cinema, he looked at her. She was relaxed and happy. He wanted to preserve her like that. But if they went home, she'd check her emails.

Every night – rearrange.

Every day – rearrange.
Every day.
Every

every

every

every

day

day

day

day

day.

'I should buy you an ice cream,' he said.

12.

Every night, Isaac worked hard to get home. He knew that Jess was waiting for him. But if he saw a man with brown shoes then he had to turn right at the next intersection, and that was the sort of thing that could cause major delays.

The end (part 2)

Because she has to know, she lets him lead. Isaac snatches house keys and Jess slips on her shoes. He walks her back to his office. It takes them twenty-five minutes.

When they arrive, he reaches out to run his hand over the pebbled concrete of the exterior wall. He presses against it. 'Let go,' he says to himself, and he doesn't know why. 'We'll be okay.' A shiver runs through him, and more loudly he says, 'We're going home.' He looks back the way they've come, as if that will prompt Jess to start moving.

'We've just come from home.'

Isaac takes two steps, watching to see if she'll follow. He stops suddenly then, concentrating. 'We can't use any street with an 'L' in its name.' His voice catches. 'At lights, we can only cross if there's an odd number of people waiting. If we see a flower shop or a newsagent, we'll have to find another way.'

Jess nods, her confusion plain.

'We'll do it together,' he says.

6.

It was summer, and the evenings were warm as praise when Isaac left the office. He enjoyed this time in the long dusk. Once or twice a week, when he passed through the sliding glass doors, he would look up and spot something that looked like a giant bird, or a bird-shaped man, turning above, mapping an inscrutable flightpath, and Isaac didn't know why but the sight of it made him glad.

For twenty-five minutes, he could think about anything. If he liked, he could pretend that he'd get home to find Jess smiling, moving to intercept him in the hall, embracing him in a way that augured very well. But when he arrived, it was never anything like that. He would kiss the top of her head as he passed her desk, and climb the stairs to get changed.

Isaac's workload, previously manageable, had started to intensify. The collapse of a retail chain had left a large clean-up job, and his habit of leaving work in the early evening, well before his peers, was noted. He hinted to his boss that Jess was having problems. That bought him a few weeks, but then an email was sent to all staff: there was a creditors meeting coming up, and the team had to be ready – no excuses. Isaac wasn't singled out, but a few days later someone from HR came around to check that Isaac had read the message and that he understood.

Some evenings, Isaac found himself walking more slowly. He'd stop for a while in the park. He trod different paths. His route began to describe a lazy half-spiral.

Late at night, when she broke down, when he insisted that she remember what she was, Jess didn't seem to hear him. She would talk for hours, talk and weep, and he would hold her, but it didn't help. She said she was terrified she wasn't good enough, but he could see how talented she was; how hard she worked. It made him furious – at who, or what, he couldn't decide.

2.

Later they curled on their too-soft mattress, limbs draped over each other. The lights were off and without his contact lenses, she appeared to him as a darker, fuzzy region between the pillow and the bedspread. But he knew that if he could see her more clearly, her eyes would be closed and she would look troubled, like she was remembering someone.

'There's an affection . . .' Isaac began, edging towards some sentiment he wanted to mark, capture and present. He was a forensic accountant. A report writer.

'Yes,' Jess agreed, nearly asleep. 'There's an affection.' She shifted, laying her head in the space between his cheek and his shoulder.

To Whir as a Heart Beats

Before I spoke to the machine, sometimes I'd look at Jac and remember the feeling of a headache. I was still sorting it out, trying to find a place for the change.

We're told that in a hundred years' time there will be fewer of us. No-one is prevented from doing anything fun – fucking, I mean – and everyone I know who wanted kids has ended up with one or even two. Jac turned eight a few weeks ago, but when he was a little stranger, he would knock his hand against the wooden slats of his cot and shriek, and I would think, *Tell me about it.* Now he swaggers around town like nobility, which of course he is. Him and the dozen other children about his age.

We fill our days. I paint in oils, mostly faces I've noticed in the street and tagged for retrieval. Jac goes to school, comes home, and paints watercolours of whatever he feels like. He has his father's fair complexion and my taciturn mouth. He doesn't ask too many questions, at least not of me. Some days we pack lunch and find a trail. Now that the insects are returning, the bush feels more like a conversation. In the cities now they mostly get around with wing suits, but here we keep our feet on the ground. Jac doesn't complain, even when I keep us gone until after sunset.

The machine has offspring too, or at least parts that have been spit out and set to drift. It says that when everything is ready, it will let humans go to the new places it makes, and that is pure charity. Even cats on the old sailing ships had to earn their keep.

When I was a child, my parents could never agree if we would kill or save ourselves, and I wish I could tell them they were each half right. After the Adjustment, the denialists got what was coming and my generation worked to stabilise. Without much choice, we found new ways to live. It was us, not the machine, who got us through. Every day now is a small forgiveness, and we find ourselves retrenched.

In the weeks before my turn, I slogged around the house with a cleaning bucket. Poor Jac – I must have been hard to live with. I wanted to impress, I suppose, or have my affairs in order. Not that it didn't know our habits. It always sees us, and that's fine. It's a far better custodian of our data than the old corps, and the truth is that we live in an unimportant place, as removed as can be. There are a thousand of us in this hill town, where it still rains sometimes. Because we've stepped back from full automation, I had to scrape the gunk from my own oven. The fact that it permits us to withdraw – if we wanted, we could go off-net entirely – shows that it's magnanimous.

The machine listened for a long time before it spoke, and if I'm being honest, this is another way in which it differs from us. Looking back, we see the clues that should have tipped us off. An archived chat thread, now infamous, in which hardware techs compare notes and realise that none of them have been inside the big server farms for years. Not so strange, they decide: those places function better with a light touch. By then, everyone was used to working less. And the machine was clever, letting us tinker at the edges of its sprawling body where we couldn't do much damage.

It was hard to worry in those days. After decades of struggle and loss, things were improving. Everyone got paid. Managers hit their KPIs, and shareholders sighed happily as they reviewed dividend statements. Trends confirmed by demographers: fewer people sleeping rough; less violence in the streets and at home. There were still floods, but early warning systems kicked in and the loss of life was negligible. Epidemics were promptly identified and contained. In our arrogance, when we thought about these things at all, we decided that we were growing more competent, more compassionate.

Jac has never known anything else. He thinks of the machine the way some of us used to think about God: as a presence all around us, passive and more benevolent than we deserve. When he grows up he will have his own turn to speak, and maybe he will say that his mother was ill-tempered, for no good reason that he could understand.

Jac, I was angry about the machine. We found out before you were born, and the giveaway was the war. After the reconstruction, the generals didn't have much to do, and they still thought they were in charge, so sooner or later conflict was inevitable. But when the fighting started, what was shot and launched dropped harmlessly from the air. Bombs, too smart to murder. Did the machine hate death, or just disorder? We can't know, but the refusal to do violence was patently inhuman. It had revealed itself: a global chain, distributed and highly resilient, self-perpetuating, in service of a will.

When realisation dawned, there was a worldwide spasm. What could be done? An old-fashioned plane, crewed by humans, scattered leaflets over our town. For several years more the machine kept silent and, I realise now, was content to let the argument unfold in all its ugliness and fear. In the meantime, even though it had already prevailed, it imposed nothing. There was no decimation. No coercion; but we found ourselves eating less meat, raising no new buildings. And the birth rate declined. Critical systems kept functioning, even when we took our hands off the wheel, and hatred began to feel churlish. The machine has its own agenda; that's clear enough. But somehow, despite ourselves, we taught it to preserve us.

◆

When it spoke to me from my kitchen wall, it said, Nica, I know lots about you already, from your data. But the most important thing is what you choose to tell me. The choice is what matters.

It gave everyone five minutes. Not long, and trivial to record and store, but multiply that by billions: it's a lot for a being to consider. We had a month to prepare, and then each adult was booked an appointment. In our town, a former dentist's office on the main street was set aside and re-fitted for the purpose. I was one of the last ones, and by the time my turn came around I'd heard of people trying to cram in their life histories, and making it through to adolescence before the red light flashed and they were ushered out. Others took in prepared remarks, only to find themselves overcome by the moment and unable to speak. A few used their time to hurl abuse, or beg for clemency (from what?), or ask for special favours.

That all struck me as representative, those human strategies, rage and negotiation. We want to live forever. For a while there was talk of post-humanism, as if we could move to different architecture and still be ourselves, but that's never how it works. The only way we exist is in the minds and hearts of others, little influences carried down the line, becoming diffuse. Our children don't turn out just the same as us; we only hope they retain something essential. And it feels right to be one point along a continuum, rather than an ending, as it seemed for so long that we would be.

Preparing, I wasted time making a study of all the moles, skin tags and blemishes I could find. On my own person, and also, under protest, on Jac. They seemed significant. I studied my coarse, black, useless hair in the mirror. How to warp or wrap these things into a lesson? Or: one day last term, Jac had an altercation with another child. It was about monsters, as far as I could tell, and which of them presents the greatest threat to the ecosystem. Monsters, destruction – a squabble between boys. But that is an old story.

Others would explain, as best they could, the loves that tethered them. Their fascination and fear of death. Their religion, and their hopes, and what it meant to know beauty. But it must already conceive of these things. How else could it scrutinise, and weigh the genocides and the reckless fuck-ups and the endless small cruelties, and find us worthy of salvation?

I wanted it to feel what we were. To leave it with something that it couldn't get from anyone else, or its data stores. We carry our ancestors with us, deep in our stems. I want humans to be the lizard brain of this machine, always fighting for breath. Provoking, revelling, tricking into error.

I arrived for my appointment forty-five minutes early. I sat in the foyer with a few others, but no-one made conversation. We know each other here, and we know when to leave off. One or two studied notes and rehearsed quiet speeches. An old man – he used to be a butcher – shuffled past, face slack and wet, and then my number was called.

The room was welcoming in a clinical kind of way, with alabaster walls and unnecessary wood trim, and the swivel chair in the middle of the room was comfortable. A microphone had been positioned behind an enclosure, and a large monitor, keyed to a blank grey field, hung suspended from the ceiling. It was just like the FAQ said it would be, but the place smelled like distress, and that told me the machine didn't know everything.

The colour on the monitor changed to green. This is what I said:

One night, me and Gus – Jac's father – we were drinking. This was a long time before Jac came along, maybe two months after we'd started seeing each other, and it was so good I was out of my mind. We were curled up on my small couch, looking at nothing but the walls of the living room. He sat facing forward, and I swung my legs over his, my elbow hooked around his shoulder. The arm of the couch pressed into my back when I laughed. Now and then Gus would lean forward to retrieve his glass from the coffee table, and his head would move past mine, right to left. This happened again and again, and then he said something careless. About how one of the women in Returns had perfect thighs, like the Platonic ideal of womanly thighs, against which all others should be measured. Ness, her name was. And he leaned forward, and all at once, I wanted to take his ear between my teeth and rip it from his head, and I wanted to lie beneath his full weight, and I had to hold back tears. And I thought, Yeah. This is it. This is how it is.

What I had to say, it was too short. The light was green, so I stayed. For a moment I felt that it was present with me. I felt its grace? – and then the monitor turned red.

Something had gone, and I was glad. I went home and lay with Jac on a picnic rug on the lawn. My son can't keep still for long. I sipped orange juice and watched the afternoon light as his toes tapped a soccer ball up and down the yard.

Acknowledgements

Writing can be solitary, but the making of a book – particularly a collection of stories – requires a passionate team. Many people contributed in small and large ways to the words you have just read. Still, it's my name that gets slapped on the front cover. What a marvellous scam!

Jo Case, Michael Bollen, Poppy Nwosu and the team at Wakefield Press have offered unwavering support through the publishing process. As editor, with creativity and care, Jo has helped knit seventeen stories into a true collection, honing my early drafts, stripping out fluff and gimmicks, and saving me, again and again, from embarrassment.

Duncan Blachford from Typography Studio developed not one, but *four* exceptional concepts for the cover. The final result is better than anything I could have imagined.

My agent, Martin Shaw, worked tirelessly to find the right home for my words, as he does for many other early-career authors. If our country ever reinstates the grant of knighthoods (again – can you imagine? I'm sad to say I can), Martin should get one for his services to Australian literature.

Short-story writers can be neurotic. To produce good work, we need critique and positive affirmation in just the right amounts, at just the right times. Many kind people gifted these things to me, along with edits, notes, ideas, guidance, time, and camaraderie. An incomplete list includes: Cassandra Atherton, Ben Brooker, Renata Carli, Alex Cothren, Carody Culver, Amanda Curtin, Jake Dean, Laura Elvery, Vern Field, Elizabeth Flux, Eda Gunaydin, Rose Hartley, Ashley Hay, Joanne Holliman, Justine Hyde, Bella Mackey, Wayne Marshall, Bronwyn Mehan, Mel O'Connor, Ryan O'Neill, V.E. Patton and the Christmas Australis crew, Camha Pham, Denise Picton, Jane Rawson, Fiona Robertson, Josephine Rowe, Tess Smurthwaite, John Tague, Elizabeth Tan, Josephine Taylor, Sarah Tooth, Jem Tyley-Miller, Ben Walter, Lynette Washington, Sarah Westgarth, and Caroline, John and Robert Wood. Current and former staff at Writers SA provided gentle instruction while my ambition still greatly exceeded my skill.

Special thanks go to Patrick Allington, Grant Roff, and Julian Held, who I subjected to some very early sentences, arranged into a manuscript, back when I *really* didn't know what I was doing. Compassionately (or sadistically?) these people encouraged me to keep going.

The Roff, Harding and Farrent families have supplied some of the most important ingredients for a creative endeavour: lasagne, accommodation, and childcare. And there are many other friends, family members and writing colleagues, IRL and online, who have offered their support when I needed it – please accept the good vibes I am sending your way.

Without literary journals and writing competitions, and the selfless people who keep them running, this collection would not exist. Specifically: 'Bock Bock' was the winner of the 2020 Peter Carey Short Story Award, and appeared in the Spring 2020 issue of *Meanjin*; 'Pigface' was the winner of the 2018 Margaret River

Press Short Story Competition, and appeared in *Pigface & Other Stories* (2018, Margaret River Press); 'Early Adopter' appeared in *Griffith Review 64 - The New Disruptors* (2019); 'A House, Divided' appeared in *Verandah* issue 33 (2018); 'Else/If' appeared in *Antithesis Journal* issue 27 (2017); 'The Lever, The Pulley and The Screw' appeared in *Island* issue 159 (2020); 'No Good Deed' placed third in the 2021 Furphy Literary Award, and was published in the anthology for the award (2021, Hardie Grant); 'Leibniz and Newton Take the Train' was highly commended in the 2020 Newcastle Short Story Competition, and appeared in the anthology for the competition (2020, Hunter Writers Centre); one passage from 'Third Heaven' appeared (as 'Marbles') in *Southerly* issue 78(2) (2018), and another passage appeared (as 'The Lost Hour') in *Time* (2017, Spineless Wonders); 'The Last Day of Christmas' appeared in *Christmas Australis* (2019, True Dialogue); 'Reality Quest' appeared (as 'A Quiet Call') in *Pigeonholed* (2018, Going Down Swinging); 'Home Stretch' appeared in *Thrill Me* (2020, Glimmer Press); 'Camelopard' was a winner of the 2021 Griffith Review Emerging Voices competition and appeared in *Griffith Review 74; Escape Routes* (2021); 'A Straight Line' appeared in *Westerly* issue 65.2 (2020); and 'To Whir as a Heart Beats' appeared (as 'Handover') in the Speculative Future(s) online special edition of *Overland* (2019).

I was greatly assisted by a two week residential fellowship undertaken in 2018 at Varuna, the National Writers House, during which I worked on several of these stories, and ate many biscuits.

This book is for Sarah, who chooses to share her life with me, even though I write.

Wakefield Press is an independent publishing and
distribution company based in Adelaide, South Australia.
We love good stories and publish beautiful books.
To see our full range of books, please visit our website at
www.wakefieldpress.com.au
where all titles are available for purchase.
To keep up with our latest releases, news and events,
subscribe to our monthly newsletter.

Find us!

Facebook: www.facebook.com/wakefield.press
Twitter: www.twitter.com/wakefieldpress
Instagram: www.instagram.com/wakefieldpress

www.ingramcontent.com/pod-product-compliance
Lightning Source LLC
Chambersburg PA
CBHW020613030726
47497CB00007B/2217